I0731786

LUNAR ALCHEMY

RISE OF MAGIC
BOOK 3

STEFON MEARS

Thousand
Faces
Publishing

Also by Stefon Mears

The Rise of Magic Series
Magician's Choice
Sleight of Mind
Lunar Alchemy
Three Fae Monte
The Sphinx Principle
Double Backed Magic
Mercury Fold (forthcoming)

Cavan Oltblood Series
Half a Wizard
The Ice Dagger
Spells of Undeath

Power City Tales
Not Quite Bulletproof
No Money in Heroism

Standalones
The Hireling
The Captain's Cat
Save Whiskers!
The Ogre of Threepeaks
Between the Cracks
Sects and the City
Prince of a Thousand Worlds
Devil's Night
Portal-Land, Oregon
Stealing from Pirates
Fade to Gold
With a Broken Sword
Twice Against the Dragon
The House on Cedar Street
Sudden Death
On the Edge of Faerie

Short Story Collections
Spell Slingers
Twisted Timelines
Longhairs and Short Tales: A Collection of Cat Stories
Dangerous Space
Confronting Legends (Spells & Swords Vol. 1)
The Patreon Collection, Vol. 1-8 (Vol. 9, coming soon)

Nonfiction
The 30-Day Novel and Beyond!

Spells for Hire Series
Devil's Shoestring
Zombie Powder
Spirit Trap
Dragon's Blood

The Telepath Trilogy
Surviving Telepathy
Immoral Telepathy
Targeting Telepathy

Edge of Humanity Series
Caught Between Monsters
Hunting Monsters

Jumpstart Duchy Series
Into the Torn Kingdoms
The Dragon's Gold
The Gift Castle
The Deadly Feast
The King's Test
Triumph in the Torn Kingdoms

Published by Thousand Faces Publishing, Portland, Oregon

http://1kfaces.com

Copyright © 2023 by Stefon Mears

Starfield image © Ashestosky | Dreamstime.com (File ID: 11418999)

Moon illustration © Olga Kurbatova | Dreamstime.com (File ID: 145496119)

ISBN: 978-1-948490-17-7

LUNAR ALCHEMY

The year is 2026
Six decades after the Rise of Magic

1

"NORTH IS A DEAD MAN."

Edik Barshai clenched his fist and watched *The Sparrow* close its feathered hatch for lift off, with a full load of tourists that should have been his. Eight wide-eyed Terrans, all ready to sail up into the air above Kennedy Spaceport and hear all about the settling of Earth's moon and view the sites of interest around the spaceport city from a comfortable distance.

Anger tightened slowly up Edik's arm until his shoulder was shaking. He should have been smelling their money right now. Not the ginseng-mint herbal odor of that alchemical solution North called fuel. Edik should have been selling them drinks and settling them in for his spiel about safety and fun.

And Edik included two sites in his tour that North overlooked. The Pillar and The Failed Site. The tourists weren't even getting as good a deal. But North, it seemed, had learned one of Edik's father's lessons better than Edik had: better service may *keep* clients, but the better salesman *gets* clients.

No. This wasn't salesmanship. Edik had already *made* the sale. North must have met the tour group on their way to his bay. Told them lies, or threw in some kind of discount. Anything to get that group onto his ship.

Still, Edik couldn't help imagining his father, shaking his head at yet another of his son's failures. Bitterness twisted through his guts as North's airship — a recent design following the unimaginative fashion of ships that looked like actual, living birds — chirped a loud imitation of a real sparrow and stood.

Edik had heard real sparrows back in San Francisco. He found the ship's performance pale and weak.

Nevertheless, Edik's black jacket and short, blonde hair were blown back by *The Sparrow's* single flap of preparation. The cold air swept past the buttons of his light blue shirt and shivered along his chest. Then the airship soared off of the blue-gray stone of Bay Two-Sixty-Two Cee, through the open hole in the ceiling above, and into the pale green sky.

Gone. They were gone. Along with money Edik had been counting on.

Edik tugged on his Van Dyke beard. He spat.

North probably saw Edik from the cockpit. Probably smiled and waved, the fare-stealing bastard.

But Edik would wipe the cocky grin off that pasty face all right. And maybe do a good deal more.

Fare stealing. Was there anything lower?

Beside Edik, the meter-tall translucent gray cat sighed and twitched his thick tail. This was Edik's familiar, Dola, and Dola's short fur didn't appear to be disturbed by the sudden breeze.

"Terrans are usually good tippers, too," said Dola. He spoke with a Russian accent, the way Edik remembered his father's voice from childhood, before time and practice had worn it down.

Dola's accent had been the first thing Edik noticed when he finally — on his third attempt — successfully summoned a familiar during the final exam of Conjuration 101, back at City College of San Francisco, the first community college in the Bay Area to have an Associate's level curriculum in Thaumaturgy.

The gray cat had faded into being with a ripple of fur, and spoken his initial greeting in English that turned *th* sounds into *z*, and made *di* and *ti* sounds as though a *y* had been inserted. Just like Edik's father.

The resemblance ended there, though. Ivan Barshai's voice had been deep and rolling. Dola's was high and, well, feline.

Edik looked about for something, anything, to vent his anger on. But the bay was empty now, a wasteland of a blue-gray cylinder thirty meters across and ten tall, with the bay number 262C in huge, pale green block letters.

Not so much as a crate or a rag left behind, and any Port Authority checkers long gone.

North's office — Northbound Tours — had to be nearby, though, and *somebody* had to be minding the shop. Edik checked the saber hanging from his belt scabbard.

"You aren't *actually* going to kill anyone," said Dola, and Edik was pleased to hear doubt in his familiar's tone.

"Within my rights." His voice was tight as he watched *The Sparrow* bank to starboard and vanish from sight. "Stealing passengers has to count as a moral crime, doesn't it? I had an agreement with those people."

"That's a— look at me, Edik, please." Dola waited until Edik met those cerulean eyes with his own hazel ones. "That's a question for a lawyer. Please tell me you won't do anything rash."

That wasn't worth a response. Edik spun on the heels of his shiny black, knee-high boots and strode toward the broad archway that led back into the port. Dola trotted to keep up with the determined click-click of Edik's heels.

"Edik, please," said Dola, trotting ahead and trying to catch his eye again. "Didn't you always ask me not to let you do anything stupid?"

"Going broke isn't smart."

"You aren't broke yet."

"I'm pretty damned close."

Edik passed through the arch and into the halls of the local traffic section of the spaceport. None of those big passenger liners here, much less the huge commercial transport ships. Nothing that advertised during sporting events or shadow plays. In this part of the spaceport were the long-term arrangements for private transportation. Airships mostly, like North's, but a few helioships like Edik's own *Third Son*, which were capable of getting from planet to planet.

Technically Edik's ship was a runabout-class helioship, which meant it was one of the smallest things flying that could brave the dark of space. And it was still bigger, flew smoother, and had more comfortable seats than that sky rat that North flew.

Unfortunately, helioships were also more expensive to maintain. Cut his margins and made him vulnerable to bastards like North.

Edik felt his jaw clench, his teeth grit tighter.

Typical crowd for this area. A half-dozen local pilots he recognized in black or blue mock-uniforms that impressed the planet-bound. They must have seen the look in his eye, though, because not a man nor woman of them raised a hand in greeting. Each got suddenly very interested in re-checking the memoboards they carried, or must have forgotten something back in the landing bay, the way they turned and hurried off.

A pack of cargo haulers in those beige jumpsuits smirked at Edik, like they would have followed him to watch the show if they hadn't been on the clock. No fear though. These were big men and women, with short hair and muscles hardened by getting crates from point A to point B, over and over. He could smell the sweat of their morning work as he passed.

Edik let them stare. Let them have their fun. He knew they'd be out of work all too soon, when those thaumaturgic lifters used in San Francisco made their way up here. Couldn't be more than another year or two. Edik had already seen them in a couple of of the richer private bays.

"Edik," said Dola, shifting sides so Edik had to look away from the haulers to see him, "this is folly. What's done is done. If we head to the city center we could still round up another group for after lunch."

"I've got that charter flight to the Romanov place after lunch," growled Edik. Not much of a fare. Most likely one-way, because the Romanovs didn't like third-party pilots hanging around their estates when they could fly businessmen back to the port and expense it themselves.

But Edik charged an honest fare and didn't hide his rates. His father would have told him to charge more for one-way than just half the round-trip rate, but damn it, Edik was not his father.

A pair of customs agents, easily spotted by the sniffer wands they carried and their blue jumpsuits with white sliver moon symbols on the shoulders and over the heart. Recent high school grads by the look of them, skinny and wide eyed, and completely absorbed in each other. The boy looked like he put effort into bronzing his skin, but the girl had a hereditary edge on him in that department.

"Hey," said Edik, pointing his steps at them. "Northbound Travel. You know it?"

"Sure," said the girl, voice still so open and unconcerned she couldn't have been on the job more than two weeks. "They fly out of Two-Sixty-Two—"

"I know where their bay is. Where's their office?"

"Back in the port?" said the guy with a shrug that might have been impressive if he'd been old enough to have shoulders.

Edik gave them a tight smile. "I know you kids are new here. But you must have spotted that this place is pretty big."

"Sure is, I'm from Jackieville, and—"

"Their office?"

The young, probable lovers looked at each other and shrugged. It was the girl who spoke. "They don't send *us* to the private offices. We're just—"

"Fine," said Edik, past them and already forgetting them like a dream he didn't care about. The office would be listed. He'd find the listing, and then...

"Come on, Edik," cajoled Dola. "At least wait until North is back. *He's* the one you're mad at."

"They need to know," he said, rising bile tightening his voice.

"They need to know they're working for a fare-stealing bastard. Unless they already know. Wouldn't be the first shady thing that man's been accused of. Just the worst."

Edik punched his palm.

"And if they know, then they're just as guilty."

2

AH, KENNEDY. CARL JONES' FAVORITE SPACEPORT. IF HE HAD TO WAIT for an attempt on his life, it might as well be here.

Bustling and noisy with the sounds and smells of thousands of people making their way through, on business or pleasure or for personal reasons that didn't fit either of those categories.

But in that way, Kennedy was like other spaceports. And Carl had seen most of them in service to Earth. For the unpredictable, he favored New Leningrad on Mars, where the corporations were turning the city into a new wild west. To marvel at a sheer, teeming mass of humanity, no place beat Kyoto back on Earth, so busy that standing still anywhere outside of designated waiting areas warranted fines. And for that new port smell, there was that place on Venus ... what was it called...

Oh. Right. Gilgamesh. How could he have forgotten? He'd read that epic a dozen times as a kid. Mostly temporary buildings yet in that port, and little traffic, but a spicy hint to the air and a sense of the exotic. The untouched. So recently settled that Earth's navy still monitored ships coming in and out. Not a popular choice with the settlers.

But Kennedy had character.

It started with the canvas — that awful blue-white stone that was cold to the touch and hard enough that Carl had yet to see a chip or scar anywhere on the walls and floors.

And he'd looked.

Old Zachariah, Carl's former partner and mentor and still a good friend — or at least, as good a friend as he was allowed to be, since Zachariah was still on the job and Carl had gone freelance — Zachariah said that the stone got scuffed and marked all the time, but that local alchemists knew the trick of restoring it as though nothing bad had ever happened to it.

That was Kennedy in a nutshell. The first human settlement away from the planet of our birth, and so proud it wanted to deny that anything could ever go wrong here. They didn't go so far as to censor their news or stifle speech — checking on *that* had been a six-month assignment for Carl and Zachariah back in the day — but they did their level best to make sure you had to look to see the rough spots.

And yet, their spaceport was...

There were more restaurants in the port itself than in the rest of the city. Enough that even though Carl lounged at a bistro table just outside a little café called Zira's, he could smell curries and rich meats and he was pretty sure he could pick out two kinds of fried plantains. Made him feel as though his strong cup of coffee was served after a tasty meal that didn't leave him overfull.

Ethiopian and Moroccan food had some popularity back in the San Francisco Bay Area, but here in the port alone Carl could choose from Nigerian cuisine, Congolese, Ugandan, even Angolan, which would have made Carl's grandfather smile if he'd lived to see it.

Grandfather said that the family's roots went back to Angola. In his honor, Carl ate there at least once every visit though, to be honest, he had yet to find a meal there he really liked.

Carl hadn't eaten there yet this trip. He'd feel bad about that if he died today.

The last time he counted, Carl had spotted restaurants in this spaceport catering to seventy-five different ethnicities, fifteen of which were African. Suited the population of Kennedy, many of whom had jumped at the chance to settle somewhere away from the history of racial tensions Carl's grandfather had gone on about whenever the mood struck him. Which was often.

The ethnic make-up also showed in the naming of the cities up here. Kennedy might have been first, but King was third, after a man so important just before technology fell, followed shortly by Newton, after the man so instrumental in holding Oakland together during the dark early days of the rise of magic.

Honestly, the place might have been mostly black if the Russians hadn't tried to take over. With their "great families" so big and important the law didn't quite apply to them the way it applied to everyone else.

In fact, a Russian was the reason for today's murder attempt.

Well, "murder attempt" might have been too strong a phrase. At least, legally. But as far as Carl was concerned, the legal ground for the claim was specious. Plus, even after all his years in the service, Carl still took attempts to kill him personally.

Among the tourists, Carl spotted recognition in a man he'd never met before. Had an eastern European look to him. Pale, with a bushy mustache, and short black hair that must have won every fight it ever had with a brush. Slender. Not muscled like Carl, but probably wiry-quick.

The guy dressed to the stereotype. Black suit, with a black shirt and black tie. Much less interesting than Carl's own muted purple work shirt and navy blue slacks, with a black belt and matching loafers.

The pale man wore his saber at his side like it was just part of the suit. *That* was worth noticing. Plenty of the tourists and business types wore "dueling swords" with that slight awkwardness that said they'd never drawn steel anywhere outside of a fencing *salle*. The pale man also had small scar on the left side of his chin and — Carl couldn't be sure from this distance — he thought the guy had scars on his hands, much the way Carl did. Probably got them the same way.

Add to all that the fact that he was walking steadily toward the table Carl sat at, moving through the crowd with a rhythm and sense of timing that made it seem that they parted for him.

No doubt then. This was the guy.

Carl stood, stretched his arms. Loosened his rapier in its scabbard. He tossed enough money next to his cup to include a generous tip and took three steps away from the table, in the direction of his would-be killer.

Whatever this guy's orders, he'd better not hurt anything at Zira's. Not the staff, who were friendly enough to seem to actually like their jobs, and even remembered Carl's order between visits. Not the customers, who were just bystanders coming in for good coffee and even better French pastries.

Not even the furniture. At Zira's the bistro-style tables were actual terran wood, stained deep red to go with the dark red café interior, and all the little accents and trims were a golden shade of brass. Surrounded by the monochromatic blue-white stone of the spaceport, it was like giving Carl's thirsty eyes a deep drink.

Carl rolled his wrists as the man came to a halt. Seven paces away, of course.

"You are Carl Jones, of Oakland, California, United North American States?" The man had an accent, but thin, as though he'd lost it and started to regain it. Slowly. Just a little trill to the *r* and a swallowing of ending consonants.

"Pretty sure you know that," said Carl.

"I require confirmation, please."

Carl sighed. "That's me."

"Thank you. And I am Matei Negrescu. I stand as champion for Alexei Lukyanov, father to Anna Lukyanova."

"If this is about Anna, why does her father need a champion? She's over eighteen, she could hire her own." Carl snapped his fingers. "Oh, that's right. Because *she* doesn't feel wronged. The claim has no merit. Walk away."

"I understand," said Negrescu, with more sympathy than Carl expected. Professional courtesy, perhaps. "However, Anna was to be married to Vasily Romanov. But when news of the affair reached the Romanov family—"

"They canceled the marriage and now Lukyanov feels insulted."

"Not merely insulted," Negrescu said with a slight shake to his head. "He accuses you of harming his family's honor and future, which *is* a moral crime under the Lunar Code. I have been sent to restore his family's honor, and perhaps the marriage."

Carl muttered, "I told her it was a bad idea."

Negrescu drew himself up straight and clicked his heels together once.

"As champion of the Lukyanov family, I challenge you to a duel to settle this matter."

"This is the best kind of gig you can get?" Carl scratched his cheek. "You move pretty well. If you're looking for more worthwhile work—"

"I have been the Lukyanov champion for ten years."

"I get it, I get it," said Carl, hands coming up. Those words might have been true, but Carl knew an excuse when he heard one. "So you're telling me you're pissed at me too." He looked closer at Negrescu's blue eyes. No. That wasn't anger. It was...

"Crap. You wanted her for yourself, didn't you?"

"You have sullied the great beauty of the Lukyanov family."

"I can't talk you into settling for first blood," Carl said a slow, shake of his head, "can I."

"To the death."

Carl sighed and drew his sword.

3

Northbound Tours didn't have its own office. It shared a reception room and receptionist with four other small companies, but Edik didn't care which ones. The shared office looked like every other one Edik had seen in Kennedy. Must've been part of the lease.

The walls were unpainted blue-white stone, though they had great, sweeping still images of space for color. Reds and greens and yellows of deep space, with stars and planets filling in the details.

Too many. Made the walls look busy. North couldn't even decorate right.

Four pale green couches for people who had to wait, including a young couple thumbing through some kind of brochure. Two yellow, ceramic coffee tables positioned for easy reach from anywhere on the couches.

The place smelled like coffee and crullers from a table behind the white ceramic reception desk.

Seated at the desk an efficient-looking young man, crisp white shirt a stark contrast with his dark skin, and making his dark blue tie more stylish than anything Edik owned. The kind of guy who probably had creases in his pants and spoke without contractions. He looked up from a refillable book.

"Yes?" he said, professional smile in his voice and on his face. "With whom is your appointment, sir?"

"Just need to poke my head into Northbound Tours," said Edik, not breaking stride. Next to him, he would have sworn Dola gave the receptionist a feline shrug.

"I'm afraid that is quite impossible, sir," said the young man, standing up and moving to intercept.

Yep. Creases in his pants.

"Look." Edik stopped and gave the kid a dark glare that came just this side of his serious glower. "You seem like a nice kid. The kind with a future. Let's not shorten that any."

"Sir, if you meant that as a threat, then I will have no choice but to remand you to the custody of the Port Authority."

"I'm here about that fare-stealing bastard Roger North, and—"

"Captain North is—"

"That fare-stealing bastard only flies an airship. Call him 'captain' again in my presence and I'll pull your tie until something pops."

"*Mister* North is out of the office at the moment, I am afraid."

The kid didn't miss a beat. Hardened spacers had turned away from the look in Edik's eye, but this kid didn't even flinch. Edik couldn't stop a smile from quirking his lips. He tried to shake it away and started chuckling. Next to him Dola heaved a sigh of relief.

"What's your name?"

"My name is Edmund McCutcheon."

"Edmund, you are too good to waste on reception work. What do you want to do with your life?"

Edik's change of mood came too quick for young Edmund, and his brows crinkled in befuddlement. His next words came out slow, but his tone stayed level, bless him.

"I am studying accounting, sir. I hope to one day be a purser."

"I do my own bookkeeping, but it's not my strength. If you come work for me, you can help with the books, then when you get your degree I'll make you a purser. It's a small ship, and I can't afford to pay you much right now" — said the man who might go out of business by week's end if he didn't find steadier revenue streams — "but you'll get some space under you as a purser, which will help if you want to go to one of the big liner companies later."

Edmund stared, like a fare who wanted the tour, but suspected a catch was coming. Edik considered saying ten different things, but tossed them all out.

"Tell you what, you check around about me. Captain Edik Barshai of the *Third Son*, and I'm a proper captain because *my* ship's a helioship. I own and operate Firebird Travel. You can let me know later if you're interested."

"I will ... keep that in mind."

Edik saw the look now. The fare was interested, but not convinced yet. Edmund would check around, hear the good things and the bad things. But he wanted that title. Edik would hear from him again.

"I cannot, however, allow you to barge into Northbound Tours without an appointment."

Edik tilted his head to the side.

"Not even if I said I wanted to book a flight?"

The kid didn't blink.

"Your behavior suggests that such a claim would not be honest. Although, if you were to say so, I would ask you to be seated while I contacted a representative about you. Any further action would require their approval."

Edik chuckled again.

"Never mind that. You have a memoboard I can leave them a note on?"

"Of course, sir." Edmund started to move, but hesitated. "If you would be so kind as to join me at the desk?"

Edmund waited for Edik to move first, and Dola nodded approval. Once Edik and Edmund were back on opposite sides of the desk, Edmund produced a memoboard. Decent size, some twenty-five centimeters long and fifteen wide, with a stylus that resembled a raven quill.

Edik wrote a full account of the situation as he understood it, and mentioned that if North did not make reparations, Edik would consult an attorney.

"Much better," muttered Dola. With one gray paw, the familiar took a recording of the text for later perfect transfer to one of Edik's own memoboards.

"Here." Edik handed the memoboard back to Edmund, the text still open so the kid could read it. "Please give this to them immediately."

And with that, and unspent anger still twitching through his arms, Edik spun on his heels to leave, passing the wide-eyed tourists without sparing them a glance. He was almost out the door when Edmund asked, "Captain Barshai, if Roger North is not a captain, what it the proper term for him?"

"He's a skipper. Anyone who commands a vessel is a skipper. But properly speaking, he's not a captain until he's commanded a helioship."

"Thank you."

Edik nodded, and as he turned away he said to Dola, "And if I don't hear from that bastard soon, he's a dead skipper."

4

Five paces.

Back in the U.N.A.S., seven paces between champions was standard. Same with Europe. Carl preferred that distance. More time to assess between the first step and the initial strike. Those extra two paces could mean the difference between ending a duel in five seconds and it dragging on for two minutes.

But here on *Luna* there was no standard. All decisions, from seconds to judges to the distance between duelists, were left to each city or town level. Kennedy kept space at a premium, so duelists started only five steps apart, and the crowd could stand as close as five meters.

And there was a crowd, of course. A burbling, sweaty crowd, filling the air with their perfumes and colognes, and their fresh coffee from Zira's, purchased to enjoy while two men tried to kill one another.

Carl loved and hated the crowds that gathered for duels.

He hated their vicarious thrill. That those who would not, could not risk their own lives to defend something they considered precious had no problem standing spectator as others did just that.

And yet, to Carl's shame, he reveled in the attention. For so long he had worked only in the shadows. Secret investigations in half-lit rooms. Working his minor talents for magic to their limits to slip past wards in two directions, gathering information his own government would deny. Fighting, even killing, to defend himself or his mission in rushed, furtive moments on catwalks or in still, otherwise empty buildings.

No celebration for his victories or sympathies for his failures. Not even real praise for his efforts, only the importance of his findings.

Now his work was in the open.

Now he stood on the blue-white stone of a public spaceport, with a high, arching dome above him that would echo the sounds of two swords clashing for hundreds of meters. Every hush or exaltation of the crowd would press on him and draw more curious onlookers.

And when the end came, he would either bleed to death while rushed medics attempted to preserve his fleeing life, or he would stand tall while the crowd applauded, loving and hating their adoration.

Carl looked across the five-pace distance at Negrescu. He remained standing still, a figure all in black with his feet together, saber naked in his hand, but point down. And the man had a fine weapon. Clean steel with the slightest curve, golden hilt with a single, elegant ruby at the crossbar. Carl couldn't see the maker's mark, but the ruby made him suspect the sword was a Dalca.

Dalca made fine blades, with a reputation for speed.

Carl's own feet were apart, his pose more casual. And the point of his own rapier down. No gold on his sword. Steel blade, steel crossbar, and steel handle wrapped in Irish linen. The only decoration was a small, faceted sapphire.

"I know," he said, "that I am a named party in this conflict, but that does not change the fact that I am a licensed champion, just like you. By law that means we—"

"Before witnesses I decline the offer of the champion's option to reduce the challenge to either first blood or first to yield." After a moment's hesitation, Negrescu gave a quick nod. "But the offer is honorable, and I thank you for it."

"We could call for a judge. Give us time to talk this over before—"

"Despite the presence of so many witnesses, you would be within your rights to call for a judge. But neither time nor words will change my mind."

"You're sure?"

Carl turned his wrist so the maker's mark on his own blade caught the light — an elaborate capital *D* with a tiny *e* in the upper right hand corner.

Negrescu blinked.

"That sword is a DeGarmo?"

Carl nodded.

A few people in the crowd whistled respectfully, and the buzz of explanation moved among them. Anyone who knew anything about dueling knew the work of Alonzo DeGarmo, the finest swordsmith in Earth's western hemisphere. Perhaps the world. Certainly no swordsmith in the colonies could match his work.

And DeGarmo only made swords for masters.

"Then I look forward to the challenge. I have never petitioned the master of smiths for a blade."

"Neither have I," said Carl. He shook his head. "Very well, let's get this over with. *En garde.*"

The crowd hushed.

As one, both men saluted with their blades and shifted side-face, swords rising. Negrescu's left hand rose high behind him, in the fashion of those duelists of yore who needed to carry lanterns in their off-hand to duel at night.

Carl's own left hand hung behind him, fingers twitching awareness of the nearest knives concealed in his belt and his pant-leg. Not that he would draw them once a formal duel had begun, but old habits clung like the dying.

They advanced at the same time, one step each. The very edge of range now, where the tips of their swords could touch. Negrescu's grip looked French. Carl noted to mix in more Italianate attacks.

Negrescu came in hard, blade flashing and drawing an "ooh" from the crowd. High then low then high then low, always leading with the point. Carl held back on defense, yielding a single step while parrying five, six, seven strikes in quick succession.

On the seventh, Carl beat Negrescu's blade aside and spun, checking his left hand from drawing a stiletto and opening the man's kidneys.

Then the moment was gone, and Negrescu back on the attack, more rapid strikes. Carl cursed as he gave ground again, barely keeping the other man's tip at bay. Too many fights lately and not enough duels. Not enough time in a *salle*. Not enough recent training.

Habits that kept him alive in private fights might get him killed in a formal conflict. But this was no time to appreciate irony.

Carl beat harder with his parries, forced an opening for a riposte in Negrescu's flurry.

The parry came slow. Carl had barely managed a stab at the man's shoulder, but Negrescu only just managed to avoid the first touch of the fight.

No wonder he fought so hard to stay on offense.

Carl held back on defense, yielding another step, then another, and forcing the crowd to move back behind him. He could hear their murmurs, their hushed speculations, but had no time for their content.

He willed his wrist to stay relaxed. To parry with twitches, not effort. All the while, waiting, waiting.

Negrescu finally feinted a low strike to set up a high thrust. But he waited too long. Carl had read the false commitment in his eye.

The low feint came and Carl shifted his weight forward as he minimized his unneeded parry.

Negrescu came high with his first slash of the fight, going for the jugular.

But Carl's neck wasn't there.

As Negrescu raised his blade for his true attack, Carl continued his momentum forward ducking low and thrusting. Up under the rib cage, straight through the heart and on into the lung.

Negrescu staggered.

Carl came up and caught the man around the back of his neck, coming chest to chest, and watching the light die in Negrescu's eyes as blood gushed out over Carl's crossbar and wrist.

Fourth lesson from his field training: always watch your enemy die, so you never forget you're killing a human being.

"I'm sorry," Carl whispered to the dying Negrescu. "I wish we could have found another way."

To their credit, the crowd had the good taste not to applaud.

5

WITH THE MORNING'S FARE A DISTANT MEMORY, AND HIS IMMEDIATE desire for vengeance thwarted, Edik passed the morning doing the part of work he hated most: filling out forms.

Firebird Travel had an office smaller than the pilot's cabin on Edik's ship. It had enough room for a ceramic desk — faux wood with fake gold trim, chimerical workspace open to display three forms in the air in front of him — a roller chair for him and two decent armchairs for clients. Edik kept a coat rack in the corner behind him, and hoped his window — his actual window, which had a view of a landing bay used by much larger and more impressive helioships than his own. Passenger liners that ferried hundreds of people to Earth or Mars, and maybe someday soon even Venus. Edik had heard that that madman Captain Jacobs had made history again by proving a passenger flight could safely reach the newest colony of humans.

Edik wondered just how safe that flight really was. He'd met Jacobs once.

But the view behind his desk looked impressive to the fares, and it distracted them from the fact that his office was so small the door to the outside almost touched his guest chairs when it swung open. For similar reasons, he kept three large, still illusions on the wall, featuring aerial views of Luna, Mars, and Earth, the last of which freshened the air with the scent of a field in spring.

But such little tricks did nothing to enlarge that available space. Honestly, Edik didn't have anywhere to put Edmund, if the young man took him up on his offer. Edik would have to rent a back room from the bar next door.

"You could replace the coat rack with a small desk and connected workspace," observed Dola, once more seeming to know Edik's thoughts. "He wouldn't need much space, and you always hang your jacket on the back of your chair."

"My fares might want to hang up their coats."

"Edik, when was the last time anyone brought a coat into this office?"

Edik declined to answer, and focused instead on the forms, a choice that made Dola snicker. A disconcerting sound, coming from a cat. Even a transparent gray cat, a meter tall.

The weather of Kennedy was mild, even when it rained.

The three-note, rising trill rang out from the comm pad on the near corner of Edik's desk, and repeated as the pad itself glowed red. Grateful for the distraction, Edik placed his hand on the pad and an illusory head appeared in the air above it, facing him.

A young woman's face. Black curls and caramel skin, with smiling brown eyes. Rosita Jimenez, the morning shift operator for the port's civilian communications web.

"Mr. Barshai," she said, "I have a contact for you from Jackietown. May I connect it?"

"Please."

Edik looked away while the head morphed into a pale, older form, with long white hair and more wrinkles than Jackson had curls.

"Mr. Barshai," she said, her voice surprisingly strong and clear, considering her apparent age, "My name is Ellen Van Andel, and I represent the interested of Northbound Tours. I have received the threatening missive left by you this morning at their office, and I have it under advisement that you came to their office this morning with the intention of inflicting bodily harm."

"Doesn't matter what I was thinking," said Edik, "not even here on Luna. I never drew steel and I never raised a fist."

"Two of Northbound's clients canceled their meeting after your tirade."

"Tirade is hardly the word I'd choose."

"Nevertheless, you have frightened business away from Northbound Tours and you have created a hostile work environment for Northbound employees."

"You want a hostile work environment?" said Edik, but Dola sank teeth into Edik's wrist, just enough to attract attention, and in words that only a familiar and its person could understand, said, "Careful, Edik."

Van Andel had a patient look in her eye, clearly expecting Edik to steer into the storm.

"A hostile work environment is what Roger North created for me when he—"

"Yes, yes, you've made your accusation plain enough. And you intend to pursue this spurious claim of yours?"

"*Spurious*?"

"I suggest that you send any further contacts about this directly through my office, here at port. Cromartie and Sullivan. Perhaps you've heard of us."

Dola dented Edik's skin further, but needlessly. Edik may have hated lawyers, but even he had heard of Cromartie and Sullivan.

"You can make faces, drop names, and hurl insults all day and you won't change the facts. North took actions he will have to answer for, under the law."

"If you insist on pursuing this baseless claim—"

Edik waved his hand through the illusionary head of Ellen Van Andel and broke the connection.

"You should have let her finish," said Dola, releasing Edik's wrist. "We might have learned something."

"We have," said Edik. "North is a fare-stealing bastard who can't fight for himself."

"He may have partners. And men who cannot fight for themselves hire champions. Some law firms even have champions on staff."

"Is this your way of saying I need to sit down with a lawyer?"

"The biggest firm in Kennedy is already on your enemy's side, so yes."

"Wrong. That's a reason to skip the courts altogether and go straight for the jugular."

"A blow that leaves you covered in blood."

Edik wasn't sure what to say to that, so he went back to filling in forms for the port. And just in case, he added the new forms necessary to include travel to Venus in his potential itineraries.

Jacobs might have been a crazy old coot, but now that he'd made the trip, the route to Venus would be clear and safe soon enough. Edik wanted to be ready when the day came.

And, though Edik would not have admitted this to himself, it might be his next port of call if North succeeded in driving him out.

6

Kennedy, San Francisco, New Leningrad or Gilgamesh, the aftermath of a duel followed the same pattern. Especially when one of the duelists died.

Carl had waited, his sword still piercing the dead flesh of Matei Negrescu, until Port Authority arrived on the scene to evaluate the proceedings. Three of them, all with dark skin, hair, and eyes, two women and one man, and lithe, fit frames. Two magicians and one normal, all three in pale blue uniforms with silver, crescent moon badges, with a flare at the top on the magicians' badges.

A licensed judge would have sped the issue, but without one the local authorities had to go through all the steps.

First, they interviewed whatever witnesses waited around, six in this case, all with the look of upstanding citizens who had extra time in their travel itineraries. Two men and one woman in suits, two others in casual clothes and one woman in the mock-uniform of a civilian pilot.

There were always a few. Whether they considered it their civic duty, or they just hoped for an opportunity to be interviewed by a reporter covering the duel, or for some other reason that Carl preferred not to contemplate, there were always a few people willing to wait and recount what they saw and heard for the authorities.

And all the while, Carl had no choice but to stand there with a dead man's blood literally on his hands — and his shoes — with the accompanying smell filling his nostrils as though seeking a guilty crack to wear at his conscience.

But those cracks had worn away years ago. Carl had tried, and that was all his personal conscience required of him.

But he hated the waiting.

The witnesses didn't even really matter. Not here in a spaceport, where local air spirits memorized every scene of violence that they would transfer to the official workstations and enter into the record. Every sight, sound and smell of the challenge and fight, forever immortalized by the spirits of the Kennedy Port Authority.

But procedure was procedure, and Carl had to stand and wait, spent adrenaline making him shaky and cold. The duel kept replaying in his head, and he realized now that no fewer than six of his parries had halted killing blows. If his hand had been any slower even once...

So Carl waited there, standing on the blue-white stone, with the comfort of coffee and pastries at Zira's only meters away, but on the other side of the solar system as far as he was concerned while he waited for the Port Authority.

Once they *finally* finished with the witnesses, then they turned their attention to the body. That was a task for the normal, verifying its identity, and Negrescu's champion's license and the employer listed by tapping the official paperwork with his badge and listening to the clear ring.

Checking his sword and his person for enchantments that might have affected the duel, one way or the other. One Port Authority magician moving a tuning fork up and down the corpse and weapon, listening for telltale changes in tone, while a non-magician inspected the wound, and pulled free the sword.

The sword was checked next. Three times each by both magicians.

They still had it when the other officer turned to Carl.

"What was this about, Mr. Jones?"

"Your local sylphs were watching. Ask them."

"I'm asking you."

"Look, you've got your witnesses. You're checking the spells. This was a legal duel, and I didn't want to fight it anyway. So why not just give me back my sword and let me try to get on with my day."

Stone walls showed more expression than the officer interviewing Carl.

"What was this about, Mr. Jones?"

"Fine!" Carl flared his nostrils in a slow, calming breath before he continued. "His employer claimed I damaged his family's honor and a marriage contract or something by having an affair with his daughter. Killing me was supposed to restore that honor and the marriage."

"This would be the Lukyanov family?"

Carl nodded.

"So you had sex with Anna Lukyanova, and he objected?"

"That's the claim."

"Do you deny having sex with Anna Lukyanova?"

"I deny that it matters either way. The accusation was made and a man lost his life for it. Lukyanov chose to settle the matter with a duel, so legally there's nothing more to talk about. The truth hardly matters now."

"It might matter to the Lukyanov family."

"I've said all I'm going to say about it. If you consider that a crime, you better be sure of yourself before you charge me. Because last I heard, neither having nor not having premarital sex is a crime around here."

The officer leaned his head to one side and regarded Carl through narrowed eyes.

"The sword is clean," announced the magicians at the same time, a strange harmony that sent a chill down Carl's back.

"So can I go now?"

"But a spell lingers about the body of Matei Negrescu," said the two magicians again, still harmonizing. "We cannot yet determine its purpose."

"I'd say that's a no," said the officer. "Looks as though you have more questions to answer for me."

"Can I at least clean up? I hate the smell of blood."

The normal officer looked back at the two magicians. The slowly shook their heads.

"Sorry, that might muddle the results of the investigation."

"Of course," said Carl with a sigh.

7

ARGUING WITH DOLA ABOUT THE BEST WAY TO DEAL WITH NORTH AND his lawyer had taken Edik the rest of the morning. They hadn't resolved anything except delaying Edik's official forms, but, frankly, anything that delayed filling out forms was a welcome entry in Edik's log.

By the time the two of them finally left the Firebird Travel office, right about noon, Edik might just have time to find lunch before he was supposed to meet his fare.

And he and Dola had moved each other not a fraction. Each maintained their position about Edik's best course of action. Edik wanted to confront North, demand restitution and challenge him to a duel on the spot if he refused. Dola, on the other hand, wanted to consult a lawyer and find out if there was legal precedent that would force North to pay or risk losing his license.

Edik had to admit that the thought of North being unable to legally fly again had its appeal, but North's blood had more appeal yet.

In any event, such happy possible outcomes must have improved Edik's mood. Other pilots were willing to meet his eye now, and some even smiled and waved as he and Dola passed them. As were the office workers and others who were sufficiently accustomed to seeing Edik's face to think of him as a local, one of their own, instead of just another tourist or traveler.

The travelers and tourists, of course, didn't offer greetings, not that there were many in this part of the port. The few who noticed him stared as though he were an oddity, perhaps because he was one of the few not in a mock-uniform or an actual uniform who moved about the port as though he belonged here.

The other tourists and travelers either tended to focus on their destinations, thus overlooking him and Dola, or stare around wide-eyed at some art display or other, or up at the blue-and-white dome, amazed at the architectural wonder involved construction that could produce a pure, stone dome some seventy-five meters high at its apex.

Proved that none of them were magicians. Edik knew, and since he knew he suspected most magicians knew, that earth elementals here on the moon had an even easier time shoving and shaping rock than they did back home.

There was probably some kind of complex explanation for that, but it involved levels of math and theory that were beyond Edik's moderate education.

That was the blessing and the curse of an Initiate's level of study and training. Lots of practical information. Focusing on conjuration and the spells required for ship maintenance meant he didn't have to worry about the thousand thousand areas of magic that Edik was not likely to find a practical use for.

At least not for money. Not the way he wanted to earn his living.

But it also meant that he didn't understand the deeper depths of magic like a Journeyman or a Magister, or most of all a Hierophant. A Journeyman would probably have known why earth elementals seemed to have an easier time with lunar stone. A Magister would have understood the fine points well enough to pull off stunts like creating this dome.

A Hierophant could ... well, even the speculation of that was beyond Edik's understanding really, but it would be impressive and accomplish more tasks at once than Edik could probably manage in a week.

But Edik didn't need to move rocks around like that, any more than he needed a lawyer to tell him he was right and North was wrong.

Edik's father would have managed to get North's lawyer to drop her client. He just had that kind of gift. Edik would have to settle for the more direct approach to his goal.

Besides, a threat and duel carried significantly less financial cost than even talking to a lawyer for half an hour, and Edik could not afford to overlook that difference, whatever Dola thought of the situation.

"Excuse me," called a vaguely familiar voice through the crowd. "Captain Barshai!"

Edik turned. He was pressed for time if he wanted to eat, but his margins were cutting a little too close right now to deny the possibility of a fare.

But it wasn't a fare approaching him. It was Edmund, an eager bounce in his step that still managed not to put the slightest wrinkle in his white shirt or deep blue tie. Edik wondered if there was a trick to moving like that.

Edik stood and waited for the boy to catch up. A moment after he arrived, his scent caught up too, a spicy, mannish smell of the sort often marketed to spacers. Or rather, people who wanted to be thought of as spacers. Most of the actual spacers Edik knew, himself included, just used scent wipers.

The last thing anyone wanted on a long voyage was an identifying stink, even one that smelled good a month or two ago.

"You have quite the reputation, sir," said Edmund, "if you don't mind my saying."

"Yes," said Edik with a devilish smile, "I'm sure most of the people around here have a story about me, whether they saw it happen or not."

"How many of them are true?" Such wide-eyed innocence on Edmund's face.

"Enough." Edik shrugged, a gesture that finished the statement for him. "I need food before I meet my fare. Care to join me?"

Edik started walking through the crowd again, and Edmund caught up within two steps.

"I would be honored, sir, but I must insist on paying for my own meal. To do otherwise might make this appear to be an interview, and I would not wish for my current employers to get the wrong idea."

"What's the right idea?" asked Dola, with a tilt of his head.

"Sorry," said Edik. "Dola, Edmund. Edmund, Dola. Dola's my familiar."

"Excuse me," said Edmund with a rapid blink. "I had not realized you were a magician."

"Why else did you think he had a meter-tall talking cat with him?"

"I ... hesitated to judge, sir. It might have involved a purchased enchantment."

"Ewww," said Dola, disgust rippling through his fur.

"What *is* the right idea?" said Edik, as much to get the conversation going again as to ease the mind of his familiar.

The crowd was getting thicker now. They were getting into the better traveled portions of the port where the white noise of thousands of people moving and talking around them forced both Edik and Edmund to speak louder.

In the background Edik could hear loudspeaker announcements about flight bay information, and customs, all deep and echoing and generally unnecessary given the commonly available personal information booths where quick, customizable illusions could provide a traveler all the information he could possibly desire.

"Well, and please understand that I intend no offense, based on the comments from those who claim familiarity with your business practices, I find myself uncertain about the future of your firm."

"Smoothest insult I've ever gotten," said Edik to Dola.

"It's true," said Dola. "Sounded almost apologetic."

"Forgive me," started Edmund, but Edik interrupted him with a laugh.

"You're trying not to ask if you can count on a paycheck if you jump ship and join me. And that's a fair concern. For too long I've been squeezing the last drop out of my fuel before blending more, if you get me."

"I ... am uncertain..."

"The answer is yes," said Edik, laughter still in his voice. This was no laughing matter, but a fare never needed to know the expiration date of his license, only that he could land the ship smoothly. "I'm on the financial brink again, and yes, it's not a new place for me."

They arrived outside McEwan's, a smallish fish and chips place that featured the horribly named moonfish. Pure marketing disaster, that name. The first breed of fish grown on Luna, some kind of blend between trout and swordfish that, when roasted, had a natural garlic-and-herbs taste.

That smell was too subtle to pull in crowds. Edik had no idea how McEwan stayed in business, and just that thought brought a sideways glance from Dola. The cat didn't need to speak to tell Edik that maybe talking numbers with McEwan might give him a clue about managing his own business.

Everything at McEwan's was ceramics in primary colors. Blue for the counter, red for the tables, yellow for the chairs. Large still images on the walls of McEwan himself — a whipcord of a man with so much body hair it seemed as though the shaggy brown mess from his scalp and face just didn't know where to stop growing.

"But here's the thing," Edik said, spinning to face Edmund and straightening the kid's already erect posture. "I was in this position eight months ago and I survived. Two years before, too, when I was just starting out here with Firebird Travel. I've had my back to the wall more times than I care to count, and I don't go down easy."

Dola cleared his throat, a subtle sound that might have been keyed only for Edik's ears, because Edmund didn't even blink. Edik did, however, get to the point.

"That's why I want to hire you. I'm great at surviving, but this is a lousy long-term plan. If I'm ever really going to build a future, I need help. And that starts with the money."

Edik turned and joined the short line of tourists. He didn't have to look back to hear Edmund's crisp step join him. Edik smiled and turned, but Edmund had a serious look.

"That's a good line," said the kid, and Edik raised his eyebrows at the contraction. "And it does fit with what I have been able to ascertain about you. However, if I were to take employment with you, I risk alienating other potential employers with whom you have occasionally placed yourself at odds."

"You're better off without guys like North."

"Skipper North has something of a reputation himself, but he is not the subject of our conversation."

"So what do you want?"

"Let me examine your books. If I am satisfied that your efforts are honest and that my assistance can help you build a strong business that shall bolster both our reputations, I shall accept your offer of employment. If not, then I am afraid you will have to persuade another to come to your aid."

"You'll have to swear to silence," said Dola before Edik could reply. "Magically."

"Cat's got a point," said Edik. "I can't let a rival's employee examine my books and carry that information back with him. Not without guarantees."

Edmund checked the knot of his tie, then ran his hand down to smooth the front.

"Then let us discuss the terms of our arrangement."

<h1 style="text-align:center">8</h1>

CARL DIDN'T EVEN KNOW THAT ZIRA'S HAD AN EMPLOYEE BREAK ROOM. It was just through the storeroom that smelled of both rich coffee beans imported from Colombia, and the newer, Lunar blends that had started growing in popularity for their light taste and smell, and their gentler touch on the nervous system.

The break room itself looked like a broom closet with delusions of grandeur. Barely big enough for a scarred, rejected redwood bistro table and a folding faux-wood chair. Light came from the ceiling itself, only just bright enough to mimic the glow of dawn.

Carl sat in the chair now, and it wasn't comfortable. It poked into his back in the wrong spot, reminding him of chairs in school that always seemed to have been designed for people a good twenty centimeters shorter than he was. His right hand was still tacky with drying blood, and his right shoe might be ruined if he didn't get it cleaned soon.

And the magicians were still holding onto his sword. In another room.

Times like this Carl was glad he had his champion's license. The local cops might be arrogant enough to snatch a nice sword from some lunkhead businessman, but no way anyone had the guts to try to keep a champion's sword. Especially a DeGarmo. No one would risk the scandal.

It helped that people in power all seemed to believe deep down that they might be able to get DeGarmo to make them a sword.

They should have asked Carl. He could have told them that wasn't how it worked.

Standing before him was the non-magician officer. Watkins. Tapping his memopad with the non-writing end of his simple stylus.

"Let's talk about your license."

"Oh, let's not," said Carl. "Let's just admit that I haven't done anything wrong and let me go. I have appointments—"

"There's a spell on that body, and I find that curious, don't you?"

"Not in the least."

"Well—"

"For all I know he was carrying a preserver."

Watkins tapped that stylus again, then turned it around and made a note. Probably trying to use the pressure of silence to get Carl to talk.

Carl considered yawning.

"Preservers are common for champions to carry?" Watkins finally prompted.

"Death is always a risk," said Carl with a shrug. "Lots of champions want their bodies preserved at the moment of death because they don't know how long it will be before their family can claim their remains."

"Sounds expensive," said Watkins in the tone of a man who could probably tell Carl exactly what the going rate for a preserver was here in Kennedy.

"Wouldn't know. Don't care what happens to my body when I die."

"Then why do you think he had a preserver?"

"Never said he did." Carl did yawn now. "Just gave an example."

"Your license includes magical dueling."

Carl didn't bother replying. Watkins had his license on top of that memoboard, and Carl assumed the man could read.

"But you don't have a license to practice magic."

"Funny the way the law works," said Carl, looking at the drying blood on his hand. Some was under his nails. He'd have to scrub it out. "I can't charge anyone money to cast a spell for them, but I can charge a champion's fee to fight a magical duel."

"So you're a lawyer too?"

"Nope. Just a man who knows how the law applies to him." Carl looked up at Watkins. "Speaking of which, do you have any reason to hold me here? I've answered your questions, and your local sylphs can—"

"You're a man who can cast spells without a license. I've got a corpse out there — a corpse you made — that has some kind of spell on it. Until you're cleared of that, you aren't going anywhere."

"I don't need a license unless I want to charge money. Hell, there must be a thousand people in this port right now who had a high school class or two and can still put together a simple spell to keep a hot drink hot. Maybe one of them did something. Or maybe Negrescu had a spell of his own up. Or maybe he *did* have a preserver. There could be a million reasons—"

Someone knocked a three-beat on the door and Carl let go of his rant.

The door opened, and one of the officer-magicians poked her head in.

"The spell," she said in a high tone that sounded a lot more pleasant without her friend offering a creepy harmony, "was scrying magic. Someone wanted to know what he was doing and when. Someone watched him die."

"Any chance Mr. Jones here did it?" said Watkins.

"Unknown. The signature is not on file."

Watkins turned to face Carl. "And as an unregistered magician, your magical signature wouldn't be on file, would it?"

"Your sylphs will confirm that Negrescu and I had to be intro-duced. I didn't know him. He didn't know me. No way I could have put that spell on him. And even if I could have, why would I? I already knew right where he was, what he was doing, and when he died."

"You might have been keeping tabs on his approach."

"Your sylphs will confirm that I *saw* him approach. That I was watching the whole crowd until he came walking toward me with deliberation."

"We agree that the probability of Mr. Jones having cast this spell is extremely low," said the magician, and this time Carl could hear the slight tones of her harmonizing partner.

"All right," said Watkins, turning back to Carl, "let's talk about Anna Lukyanova."

"Let's not," said Carl, standing up. "You said I had to wait here until I was cleared of that spell. Well, it sounds to me as though I've been cleared, right?"

The officer-magician nodded.

"Then we're done here."

Carl started toward the door, but Watkins stopped him with a hand on the chest.

Carl looked down at the shorter, skinnier man. He held up his clean left hand.

"My license."

Watkins hesitated, then handed back the license.

Carl looked down at the hand still on his chest, then back at Watkins' eyes.

"Step lightly, Mr. Jones. The Lukyanov family will not let this go. They've got a lot of friends and connections around here, and they'll be only too happy to make your life ... unpleasant."

"Then tell whoever holds your leash that I don't like harassment. And I know a thing or two myself about making people's lives ... unpleasant. Now take your hand off of me or lose it."

Watkins removed his hand.

Carl started back into the storeroom where the two Port Authority magicians held his bloody sword up, presenting it to him. Carl grimaced at the stickiness of the drying blood. Between the sword and his hand, he needed at bathroom, stat.

"You'll wish you'd kept it in your pants, Mr. Jones," Officer Watkins called after him.

Carl resisted the urge to tell him the truth.

9

"THAT WENT WELL," SAID DOLA, HIGH STEPPING ALONGSIDE EDIK through the port to the public areas where Edik was due to meet his charter passenger. "Quite a reasonable settlement on terms for the *geas*. And his assessment will tell us how good he is at bookkeeping."

Edik scanned the bustling crowd, looking for ... some coffee shop. Out here where the tourists and travelers ran in thick packs in clouds of rumpled cloth and warring perfumes, spotting anything was a trick.

Making things worse were the statues. Odd-shaped edifices that varied between five and twenty meters tall, each formed out of rough white rock tinged with a sickly shade of green. Some of them were surrounded by ferns, which were themselves surrounded by blue-white stone benches.

Normally Edik liked the statues. Not their weird shapes so much, but the way they formed partitions that helped herd the crowds along the travel lines they needed to reach landing bays, or customs check points, or visitor waiting areas and ground transportation points beyond them.

But this was a terrible place to spot someone.

"Why did I agree to meet him out here?" said Edik, stopping to look around.

"I believe it's part of your exemplary service plan," said Dola. "Something about the proper treatment for private fares? Anyway, I do like that Edmund. Canny, and not afraid to call you on your bullshit. God knows I need an ally there as much as you need a good bookkeeper."

"Hey!"

Dola licked a paw and swiped it across his brow, clearly letting the statement stand for itself.

"He said something about a coffee shop. Sara's, I think? It's got to be somewhere around here."

"Zira's. And it's off to the right past the statue that looks like a bird."

"Which one is that?" Edik looked back and forth, then spotted a shape that had two protrusions straight down from the base of a vaguely cylindrical shape that leaned at a forty-five degree angle. Two slats hung behind it, close to the cylinder and following the same line. "That?"

"Of course. What did you think it was?"

"An artichoke on the prongs of a corn holder."

"You don't eat enough."

"You just see birds everywhere."

Dola ruffled his fur, but followed along when Edik started that direction, detouring around an overweight couple with a flock of children that couldn't all be theirs, if only because the mix of ethnicities.

Edik slowed. Six kids, herded by a harried looking couple. Probably just got off their transport. Getting situated before they claimed their luggage. Found their hotel. Made their formal plans...

"I see him," said Dola.

"One second," murmured Edik. Louder, to the couple, he said, "Excuse me, folks, but you have the look of a group only just meeting our beloved Luna."

The couple looked up, confused, and sweatier than Edik had realized. The kids were restless, chattering and jumping on and off the stone bench behind the couple.

"It just seems to me—"

"He sees me," said Dola, waving a paw.

"—that the best way to get to know Luna—"

"He's coming this way."

"—is from the sky. For a very reasonable price I can show you—"

"Edik, he looks like he's in a hurry."

"—all the important sites from up high above. And from there—"

"Edik..."

"—you'll be in a better position to judge the ones you want to see closer—"

"Edik Barshai?" Not Dola's voice, but a deeper one. Confident and, unless Edik was mistaken, irritated.

"The man's right, folks. My name is Captain Edik Barshai of Firebird Travel." He pushed a business card into the man's empty hand. "You won't find a better deal anywhere. The most sites for your dollar with the most details, seen from the most comfort."

That deep voice *ahem*ed pointedly.

"But so in-demand is Firebird Travel that even now I have to get moving, going the extra distance to keep my customers satisfied. Remember, folks, that's Firebird Travel, for all your airborne and spaceborne needs."

Edik turned to meet the raised eyebrow of the man who had to be his fare, Carl Jones. Tall as he'd said he'd be, even taller than Edik. And sure enough, he did have that ebon black skin that stood out even here in Kennedy. Muscled too, with scarred hands and close-shorn curls like a man of action. Carried his rapier with as much comfort and ease as Edik carried his saber.

Edik liked the man instantly.

Edik smiled and held out his hand. "Good to meet you, Mr. Jones. Let's get you airborne."

Jones started walking like he knew where the right bay was, and Edik felt a fleeting wonder again that he'd bothered coming to meet the man.

"Fly to the Romanov estate often?" said Jones, setting a brisk pace, but not an uncomfortable one for Edik. Before the pair of them, the crowd seemed to part.

"Couple of times a year. They handle most of their own transport, so the usual type I take out there are political hopefuls trying to garner favor." Edik favored Jones with an unnecessary glance at the man's purple work shirt, black pants, and especially the small blood stain on his right shoe. "You don't seem that type."

"Hell no. I'm a professional champion."

"Is this for a duel? Because if you're going to ask me to stand second, that would put me in a legal gray area..."

"Don't need a second." Jones shook his head crisply. "They want to talk to me and the topic's not yours for the asking."

"Just making conversation."

They both went silent as they passed a six-person customs team carrying their sniffer wands.

"You have any objection to staying ready to fly in a hurry?"

"You willing to take a bound oath that you're not asking me to fly you there for anything illegal?"

"If you need me to. I'm not looking for trouble. But something went wrong this morning and trouble might follow me anyway. Might need a quick exit."

"The Romanovs might not let me stay."

"I'll make them." The look in Jones' eye left no doubt that he meant those words. He might not have understood just how powerful that family was though.

"I don't argue too well facing down a security team armed with slingers."

"*They* want to talk to *me*," insisted Jones. "The only way they're sending you away is with me on board."

Dola cleared his throat.

"You do understand," said Edik, "that you only contracted for one-way travel."

"That was all I thought I'd need."

"I'm just saying that round trip, or a second destination, costs extra. Plus waiting time, if it goes more than an hour."

"Done."

Edik blinked. He'd expected an argument. Some bartering. Something.

"I like your familiar, by the way. Never could manage that myself. No talent for alchemy."

"Best fare you've had in weeks," said Dola, using words that only Edik could understand. And Edik knew the familiar wasn't talking about money.

"You think they're going to try to kill you?" said Edik. "Think you might need help?"

Jones looked him up and down.

"An hour ago I'd've said no way. Now..." Jones shook his head and looked down the passage ahead of them into the small transport section of the port.

"Now I think I just might."

10

ANNA LUKYANOVA SAT AT AN ANTIQUE OAK ROLL-TOP DESK. IT HAD TWO dozen tiny drawers that she'd found, and probably at least a half-dozen more that she hadn't puzzled through yet.

She loved this desk. It kept her secrets.

She would feel terrible if she ruined it.

Right now she had a ceramic mortar in front of her half-full of three, carefully ground and powdered herbs and roots. She had three beakers next to it on a small rack. Two of the beakers were empty, and the third was full of a clear, bright yellow liquid that was absolutely useless.

No. Not useless. Wrong, because it hadn't concocted into the proper brew. But it might yet have properties worth exploring. When she had time, which she did not just now.

Just now she was sure she had the blend right. Just now she had a decanter of fresh, natural water, strained through bay leaves and again through chicory, then left to sit for thirty-eight minutes before being poured into its current decanter.

Thirty-six drops, in twelve sets of three spaced eight heartbeats apart. That would, should, *had to*, activate the blend properly. If it gave her the right shade of green, not that stupid yellow, she could then add enough regular water to bring it up to a full quarter-liter dose.

Behind her someone had the audacity to knock.

It was a firm knock, designed to carry across the expanse of empty air to anywhere in Anna's parlor, or even on into her bedroom, should she have been reading or having a nap.

Anna grimaced and rolled down the desk-top to conceal her activities. She dusted her hands, then stood and straightened her dress, pearl white cut high enough above the knee and low enough at the neckline to be in fashion — over Father's objections — but not enough of either to be unladylike.

No jewelry, of course. That was only for special occasions, or to mark a title or position. And Anna had earned none, unlike her brothers and sisters.

She stood and crossed the soft, welcoming rug toward the ornate oak door. Enchanted, of course, for comfort and ease. As the twin facing French-style red couches had been, as had the two padded chairs by the window, perfectly positioned to catch the afternoon light and to give a view across the crater toward Kennedy.

She cast her eyes longingly at the books in her high bookcase beside the door. Histories and fictions mostly, printed back before the rise of magic, but father had allowed her two dozen of the newer, refillable books. Probably assumed she filled them with romance novels, like her sisters did.

"Yes, Father?" she said, opening the door and greeting his scowl with her sweetest tone.

Father hardly stood a score of centimeters taller than she did, but his weight and bearing lent an imposing cut to his mien. He was dressed in a black, evening suit already, which told her all she needed to know.

"Matei is dead," Father growled. "It seems your *lover* is skilled enough to carry a DeGarmo blade."

"Is he?" Anna used the impressed tone she gave Father when he mentioned some business accomplishment without giving her the details. As though she were expected to be impressed because he impressed himself, without ever sharing the knowledge that went behind the work.

"Enough of your gloating." He sniffed the air. "I..." He sniffed again.

"My latest potpourri. Do you like it? I think it's ... woodsy."

"It smells like the garden threw up. Open your windows. And do not change the subject."

"Yes, Father," Anna said, her eyes properly downcast. "I'm sorry, Father."

"You've done an excellent job of spoiling my hard work with the Romanovs. You understand that Pajari's daughter will likely get that marriage now. And the alliance that comes with it."

"Yes, Father. I'm sorry, Father."

"What were you thinking, girl?"

"The heart wants what the heart wants, Father."

Father clapped his hands, a sudden sharp sound that made her look up.

"If this were about your heart, you'd have run away with him. You spoiled the marriage to spite me."

"Father, I—"

"To think you would go to such lengths to hurt me, Anna. It breaks my heart."

Anna's stomach sank and tears welled in her eyes.

"Father, I never meant—"

"You did, child. You lay with a strange man and told yourself ... whatever you told yourself. But you did it to spoil the marriage. Even knowing how much it meant to me. To this family. To the future. Anna, you have done us all more harm than you can possibly understand, and most of all to yourself."

Anna's heart pounded in her chest. Tears were flowing freely now, without even a sob to make her shake.

"Father..."

"And you sit here in your room, day after day, and tell me you assemble potpourri? I'm not a fool, child."

Anna didn't know what to say now. The pain in her father's voice was too raw.

"You have no talent for magic. Did not your tutors convince you of that?"

"N-not for s-spells, Father, b-but…"

"*No!*" Father slashed the air with both arms. "No, you will not speak to me of alchemy. Not that low trade. What would you do, Anna? Waste yourself blending fuel for ships? Preservations for spells that keep beds soft and warm in the worst weather?"

"But, Father, I—"

"No, Anna." Father voice got quiet now. The storm spent, but she knew that the gentle tones that followed might carried the worst dangers of all. "No more."

Father put a warm, rough hand on her shoulder and leaned in so that she saw deep into his ice blue eyes, so very like her own.

"Matei's funeral will take place at dusk. You will attend, and *you will dress appropriately.* And since you have ruined your prospects for a worthy marriage, you will provide me with a list of ten ways you can work to help your family. *And alchemy shall not be one of them.*"

Anna started to speak, but Father held up a warning finger.

"I mean it, Anna. Ten things. And if I do not like the list, then *I* will choose."

He turned and stomped off down the madrone wood of the hallway.

Anna closed the door and returned to her desk. She rolled up the top and looked down at the blended herbs and root waiting in her mortar.

"But I'm *good* at this," she said to no one.

11

THE VIEW OUT THE FRONT OF THE *THIRD SON* WAS SPECTACULAR. CARL Jones had ridden on many ships in his day, but always either back where the passengers sat, or tucked away, hidden somewhere.

Stowed away, if he felt inclined to be technical. But he didn't like to think of it that way, because he wasn't bumming a ride when he did it. He was traveling as far under the radar as humanly possible, on assignment.

But never before had Carl Jones sat in the cockpit of a ship in flight.

First, it was smaller than he expected. True, the cockpit had to fit inside the head of a giant firebird, because Barshai had told him the ship was fashioned to look like the creature out of Russian legends. Of course, Barshai also called the cockpit a bridge, which Carl thought was overstating the case.

The body of the bird, where the passengers sat, was about three meters wide, but the cockpit narrowed toward the tip. Barshai himself sat as far forward as possible, his padded swivel chair at the junction of two white ceramic counters that formed a V under the huge transparent ceramic viewing area, which was where Carl was treated to magnificent views of the lunar landscape, once they'd soared past the dark yellow of the Barrier surrounding Kennedy and rendering it habitable by humans.

Barshai himself looked as though he should have been a pirate. Black pants with a silver stripe down the sides, coming out of knee-high black boots. Black jacket over a blue, button-up shirt. Wore his saber like he knew how to use it. But none of that gave him the roguish quality that made Carl think pirate. What was it...

The beard. That blonde Van Dyke on the strong chin. Played off of the short blonde hair. Gave him a slightly sinister bearing, just enough to suggest that laws were something he followed when it suited him.

The cockpit smelled of herbs and borscht. Carl could even see a crusted spot where some borscht must have been spilled on the counters. The counters themselves held all the controls of the ship. A snarl of glowing blue strands floated in the air for the communications web. The scanners showed a pair of small, illusory views of the ship's surroundings, with two glowing, golden illusory hand-grips below them for more direct control. The helm itself three phantasmal adjusters for pitch, roll, and yaw, next to an illusory red handle with settings for "ahead full," "three-quarters," "half," "one-quarter," "all stop," and "reverse." Finally, there was a small miniature illusion of a firebird that must have represented an overview of the ship itself.

Carl sat behind and to the right, on another swivel chair with its own small white ceramic counter. No apparent displays or controls though.

Not that Carl cared about the controls. He was more than happy to let Barshai do the flying. In fact, he'd looked forward to watching a pilot work. See what he could pick up, with the thought that it might come in handy someday.

But the flying itself was more boring than he could possibly have imagined.

The moment they took their chairs, Barshai had looked at him, gleam in his hazel eyes, and said, "Ready?"

The moment Carl replied, Barshai said, "Nixia!"

A small air elemental whooshed into being in front of them, like a willowy human woman with hair almost as long as her one-meter body, except that she was composed not of flesh, but of swirls of lemon-yellow air. And her hair never stopped moving. She appeared to wear a sundress of light chiffon the same color as her emulated skin.

Nixia had looked Carl over appreciatively with her orange-yellow eyes, but Barshai said simply, "We're going to the Romanov estate. Guide us there by the usual route, if you would be so kind."

"Of course, Edik," she said in a breathy voice, then dissolved right there.

The ship lifted off.

"Impressive," said Carl. "I've heard that most elementals require very specific bindings and instructions to follow out tasks."

"Like anyone else, it depends how you treat them." Barshai had turned toward the viewing area. "Want me to point out places of interest on our way?"

Carl did, and for the first several minutes of the flight Barshai had named every interesting feature immediately surrounding Kennedy. The city itself was set in the center of a great crater, and its Barrier described the edge of that crater. In fact, it was the visible edging of the crater that had given rise to the idea of a Barrier in the first place.

Most of the city and development was concentrated in the center, but they left plenty of room to grow in the surrounding environment, which meant for plenty of hiking and swimming in the interim. True, the grass was never quite green — always a little bluish and scrubby — and the water often tasted of lemon, but it was a taste of Earth here on Luna.

But now they were away from Kennedy and Carl could privately marvel at the contrast of the stars above and the yellow of the Barriers surrounding every city, town and, apparently, private estate. Though none of them as dark a yellow as Luna's first Barrier, around Kennedy.

Finally, he had to ask.

"Just how many Barriers are there on Luna?"

"Officially," said Edik, slicing a green apple for them to share,

"Just under thirty. But I think some of the private estates are trying to expand on their own."

"Whose jurisdiction do they fall under?"

"In theory, they follow the laws of the nearest city. In practice, they do pretty much what they want. Take the Romanovs, for example. Their estate is technically equidistant from Kennedy, Vladivostok, King, and Petrograd." Barshai shrugged and handed Carl a slice of apple. "So whose laws are they supposed to follow?"

"Are you trying to say they could kill us both the moment we set down and be within their legal rights to do it?"

Barshai twisted his mouth around, and looked down at his familiar, who must have said something that Carl couldn't understand.

"Wouldn't go that far," Barshai finally said around a mouthful of apple slice. "More like they'd cover it up and nobody could make any charges stick."

"Lovely." Carl bit into the apple. A little sour for his tastes, but his mother taught him never to insult a host's offerings. "So what do you do, notify your next of kin when you have to fly out there?"

"I look at it like this." Barshai settled down in his chair, both feet flat and a prosaic cast to his features. "They won't kill me because there's no money in it. They start killing pilots who fly people out to their place, pretty soon no one will do it."

"So what you're saying is..."

"*I'll* leave just fine." Barshai pointed with his pairing knife. "*You* might be in trouble."

Carl chuckled. "What's one more attempt on my life today."

"What was the first?"

Carl started to shake his head, then shrugged. No reason not to tell him. The duel was a matter of public record. He gave him the particulars in brief.

"Was she worth the duel?"

"What was my other option, let the guy kill me?"

The familiar, Dola, said something. Even though Carl watched the cat's lips move he couldn't make out a word. Whatever it said, Barshai laughed, a sound of honest humor.

"You could have let him hear that one," said Barshai to Dola. Turning to Carl, he said, "Dola, being a cat you understand, said that of *course* a man should be willing to die for good—"

Nixia swirled into being in front of them. In the same breathy tones she said, "We'll be ready to land within a minute, Edik."

"Thank you. The usual spot if it's open. If not, let me know."

Barshai spun on his chair and twisted a strand of his communications web. In the air above the glowing blue formed the severe face of a young man with black hair and a stark widow's peak.

"*Third Son* coming in, bringing Carl Jones as discussed."

"*Da*, land on the pad closest to the main house. A servant will meet you."

The connection cut and Carl looked over the grounds of the Romanov estate as the ship passed the yellow of their Barrier.

The estate was set into a rocky, dull gray hillside. But only the rocks behind the mansion itself were that color. The gold and white mansion — presumably the "main house" — had seven stories and probably hundreds of rooms, including no fewer than three turret towers that Carl could spot easily.

Rippling out from the main house were acres of lawn, a swath of forest, and just down the hillside a veritable village of smaller, brown buildings.

Carl could spot two dozen men on horseback, scattered about in twos and fours like guards on patrol, which they probably were. Just in case anyone wanted to sneak hundreds or thousands of kilometers across the lunar landscape, outside the protection of a Barrier, for the chance to sneak into the estate.

Back in the day, Carl would have air dropped further up the mountain and found an unguarded way down.

Or maybe stowed away on a ship like this one.

But Carl had no intentions of spying on anyone or killing anyone.

And he hoped that were still true when he left again.

12

As the *Third Son* touched down in the center of the crushed granite landing circle provided by the Romanovs near the edge the their first wave of lawn, Edik reflected on the joys of his small ship.

When Edik had first imagined opening his own travel business, he pictured himself commanding one of those large passenger liners. A crew of dozens. A cabin large enough to have a study, maybe. Even when he'd bought the *Third Son* — back when the maker had the audacity to misname it the *Phoenix* — he originally saw it as a stepping stone toward a larger business.

But with great size came great hassles. Right now, Edik's ship was being guided to a perfect two-claw landing by an air elemental *he* had conjured. Completely hands-off on his part.

He couldn't name a single passenger liner that could trust its landings to the hand of an air elemental. They had too many total bindings and compulsions. Too many moving parts.

"Here we are," said Edik, standing up when the ship finally settled down to its resting pose. "Safe and sound and ahead of schedule by ten minutes. I hope you'll remember that whenever—"

"Captain Barshai," said Jones with a smile, "you don't need to sell me."

He stood and offered his hand to shake. Jones had a firm, respectable handshake.

"Come on," said Edik, turning and leading his passenger out of the bridge and into the main body of the ship. A cabin-long ceiling mural of a mythical firebird's tail feather, red and blazing against the gold background of the hull interior. Beneath it, eight beautiful seats of brown leather, tanned from the hides of actual Terran cows, four on either side of the long, golden carpet of the center aisle.

Each chair padded and molded and tall enough even for Edik's two meters of height. The adjustable base meant even children could ride without dangling their feet. Three hundred sixty degrees of smooth rotation. Meter-long portholes trimmed in fiery red, one for each chair, offered fantastic views when airborne or space-borne, and a shelf below those portholes kept snacks and drinks stable.

Padded, five-way seat belts provided safety over and above even Terran regulations, which made them well beyond the requirements here on the moon.

The best accommodations for the money. Edik almost pointed them out, or the freshness of the air provided by his air elementals, but no. Jones had already declared himself sold. He didn't need another pitch.

Instead Edik stopped forward of the seats, placed his hand in the right spot on the interior hull, and said, *"Sezam otkroysya."*

A seam appeared in the hull ceramics, then a curved rectangle of a door swung open, leaving a single step down to the crushed granite. Already Edik could hear birds singing. Scores of them, at least, from the nearby fir trees.

Edik was also glad he hadn't boasted about the freshness of the air. The air here tasted even better. Over in Kennedy, where the Barrier was the oldest erected by human magicians, the air always tasted of licorice. Edik thought his elementals had gotten all of that out of his ship's air.

Apparently, he was wrong. This air tasted so clean Edik remembered hiking outside Moscow with his father, drawing gulps of air between gulps of water from a fast-flowing stream. The breeze in Edik's face now tasted just like the air above that stream.

Horses trotted past in the background, ridden by men in dark brown uniforms. By their sides they wore long, curved shashkas, the same kind of swords used by the Cossacks of old.

They might as well have had furred hats on their heads, despite the warmth of the day.

Edik stepped down onto the gravel, Jones just behind him and Dola following last. Waiting for them was a thin, elderly man, immaculately groomed from his tufts of white hair to the gleaming polish of his black shoes. He even wore white gloves.

Apparently serving the Romanovs was a formal occupation.

"Mr. Jones," the man said. No quiver of age in his voice, despite his legion of wrinkles. Merely simple assertion. "I am Leonid, and I am to escort you to the presence of Natalia Romanova."

"Thank you," said Jones, with a small bow that even Edik had to admit seemed to fit the dignity of the servant.

"Mr. Jones requests that my ship and I wait here for him. Will that be a problem?"

"It is an unusual request, sir, but I doubt it shall pose a problem as we are expecting few guests today. Nevertheless, I shall enquire and send you word."

Edik closed his eyes and sighed through his nose.

"I'm to wait here then, am I?"

"If you'd please, sir."

"Right." Edik turned to Dola. "Of course."

Jones exchanged a wave with Edik, and followed the efficient and surprisingly rapid steps of Leonid, while Edik had to wait with the ship.

"You'd think, just once, I'd get to see the inside of the place."

"The air is quite nice out here," said Dola.

"Must be like a Russian museum in there. You'd think they'd offer a tour to a guy like me, with roots going back to the same homeland."

"And there are birds. I could chase them. You know. Be a kick for you." Dola's tail twitched. "You'd watch. It'd be funny."

"Dola..."

"I'll just catch one." That tail was really moving now. "You'll see."

"Don't chase the birds," said Edik before Dola completed a single step.

Dola's tail dropped disconsolately, and his ears folded back as he gave Edik his best pleading look.

"No," said Edik. "You're not getting us kicked out of this place."

"So I have to sit here and do nothing? While they sing like that? *Taunting me* with their flavor profiles?"

"Join the club," said Edik, dropping down to sit on the lip of the hatch. "Join the club."

13

CARL EXPECTED TO BE ESCORTED INTO THE HUGE MANSION THAT gleamed in the bright, early afternoon sunlight, but instead the old servant Leonid led him across the wide expanse of lawn toward the side of the house. A shame. He'd wondered how a family like the Romanovs would decorate the inside of a white-and-gold behemoth like that. Probably antique this and antique that, relics going back to the days of the Tsars. A whole house full of things that no one was allowed to touch, much less enjoy.

Probably why an unknown like Carl wasn't allowed inside.

Or maybe he was. Maybe Leonid was taking around to the servants' entrance or something.

No. That small servants village — or whatever the Romanovs called that row of small houses just down the hill — was off to the right, so the servants' entrance had to be on that side. Leonid was leading him around the house to the left.

The grass of the lawn was so thick and plush that Carl disliked it within five steps.

Sure, it smelled good, summery in the spring air, but still. Grass should have been trimmed shorter, more evenly than this. If Carl had to fight on grass like this he couldn't trust his footing. Dew would cling too long in places. Tufts would add odd angles in others. Why would anyone...

Before he could even finish the question in his head, Carl heard his answer. The distant bleating of goats. Fresh milk, fresh cheese, occasional meat no doubt, and probably fed through lawn care. Efficient.

"Where are we going?" asked Carl, looking around. There was a grove of firs no more than a hundred meters to his left. Closer than the house. If he ended up running from any of the mounted guards on patrol, the trees were the direction to run.

Carl didn't expect to have to run, but the habits of old training were too ingrained to ignore.

"The mistress is instructing her youngest in the fine art of the crossbow. She will receive you at the range."

Crossbows. Now *those* were difficult to outrun.

Rounding the corner, Carl came close enough to the mansion now to smell the purple and yellow narcissus plants that edged the house. Old allergies — nearly forgotten from all his time spent in heavily controlled environments — itched at his nose and eyes.

He resisted the urge to sneeze, but hoped no one noticed the contortions his face went through in the process.

The clatter of a breaking plate made Carl's hand twitch toward his sword, but he calmed himself with a slow, smooth breath through his mouth. The duel had made him jumpier than he thought.

Ahead of him now, Carl could see a huge swimming pool, complete with a pool house larger than the house Carl grew up in, and the hint of a hedge established by a row of lavender, Russian sage plants.

And past that, Carl saw the woman who had to be Natalia Romanova, holding a spent crossbow with the casual ease that only came from a great deal of practice. She looked tall, maybe one and three-quarters meters, slender in a dark green dress that set off the pale blonde hair that fell past her shoulders. Her feet were apart for balance, and her matching boots disappeared inside the dress.

The boy she spoke to was in his teens, but either just into them or cursed with the wrong genes, because he still stood shorter than his mother. He had her hair, though, trimmed back to neck-length. He wore a sharp red shirt, buttoned to the neck and at both wrists, and deep brown slacks that tucked into ankle boots.

Leonid kept his steady pace, and Carl never had a chance to give the area a proper assessment. He spotted two more mounted guards down near the edge of the house. No crossbows to match those curved swords of their though...

No. Scratch that. They had hand-crossbows. Shorter range, but plenty of kick. And they might have been enchanted. Carl couldn't tell from here.

He could tell that Romanova wore something enchanted around her neck, as did her son.

Not the crossbow though. They took their training seriously.

"Madam," said Leonid as he and Carl passed the row of sage plants, "may I present Mr. Carl Jones, professional champion, here at your request." He stopped and turned to Carl. "Mr. Jones, I have the honor to present you to Natalia Romanova, and her son Ivan Romanov."

Romanova turned and Carl's breath caught. She wasn't beautiful, not the way he'd come to think of the word. Her eyes weren't just pale blue, they were the color of ice. Her face was too strong, her chin and cheekbones too severe, but the woman had a presence he couldn't deny. And he couldn't guess her age. She could have been anywhere from thirty-one to forty-five, and even that range he kept to only because of the presence of her son.

"Mr. Jones," she said in a cultured soprano that held only the traces of a Russian accent, "thank you for coming."

"Thank you for inviting me." Carl paused and did something he'd never done before. He gave a slight bow. Later he would tell himself that it was just the setting. The mansion, the servant. But deep down he knew it was just a response to the woman's sheer nobility of bearing.

The times that Carl would later consider that reason made his stomach twist with discomfort.

But in the moment he continued, "I have asked that my pilot and his ship be allowed to remain. Once our ... audience is concluded, I have another appointment to attend to."

"Of course," she said, as though she expected this, despite everything Barshai had said. "Leonid, you will send a runner?"

"Of course, Madam." The old servant bowed twice as deep as Carl had, and excused himself.

"Mr. Jones, my son is only just now willing to take up the crossbow. I realize this is late — he nears his fourteenth birthday — but at times I have a mother's failing of indulgence." She smiled. "Would you be willing to favor us with a demonstration?"

Something about that request slipped suspicion down Carl's spine. Made him want to check over his shoulder to make sure someone wasn't going to...

No. No way they would have called him out here for that.

"With all due respect, Madam, I specialize in the sword and the spell for a reason. It is the rare duel indeed that sees a combatant choose the crossbow as his weapon."

"Then you have not dueled enough women," she said. "I think you'll find that women favor the speed and surety of a single shot over the prancing and swiping of a sword."

Carl had dueled at least a dozen women as a champion, and two for personal reasons. All had chosen the sword or the spell. He declined to mention this.

"Please, Mr. Jones." She held up the crossbow. "Five shots. I think my son will find it inspiring to watch the work of a professional. And I believe we both know you have experience with the crossbow."

So that was it. She wasn't talking about his time as a champion. She was talking about his time serving Earth. But that work was strictly confidential, protected information.

Damn. Refusing would be rude, and he was a guest. It might also cost him a commission, if she wanted to hire him. But demonstrating his skill might confirm information she had gathered.

Carl sighed through his nose. He was who he was and he'd done what he'd done. He would not apologize for that.

"All right," he said, approaching and taking the crossbow.

He didn't recognize the manufacture. It had the lines of a sport weapon though, used for skeet or hunting. It lacked the clasps for holding spare bolts that a military crossbow always had. And he suspected — but declined to test the theory — that the stock was not removable and contained no blades.

But the sight on it appeared true enough.

Sitting at their feet were two quivers, one still with its full complement of twenty bolts, the other with only five remaining.

He drew one from the five, placed it, and pulled back the string with two fingers. It came so easily he might have only needed one to pull it. He tilted it to examine, and saw the mechanism — the bowstring was loose when empty, but when cocked tight, weights inside it shifted and coiled the tension to full strength.

Definitely not a military weapon. Too many moving parts.

Carl set his feet apart and looked down the field. He could see bushes with mounted bullseye targets at twenty-five, fifty, and one hundred meters. But today's targets were pristine. Instead he could see the remains of round clay targets, shattered by accurate bolts.

He could also see a small wooden block to the left side of the field, with a servant's head poking out from behind it. No doubt the man who launched the skeet.

Romanova moved behind him, which made Carl's neck itch. The boy stood to his right, silent, but eyes intent on the details of Carl's movements.

"Pull!" said Carl.

Up came the clay plate.

Carl tracked and fired, shattering it before it reached the apex of its flight.

He called for the next as he reached for a second bolt. The crossbow loaded so easily the skeet plate only just passed its zenith before it shattered.

Carl shot the next three the same way, as rapidly as he could call for them.

As soon as he loosed the last bolt, even before he heard it strike its target, he turned to the boy and held the crossbow out to him. The boy stared back at him, wide-eyed.

Romanova applauded with soft, rapid claps.

"Oh, well shot, Mr. Jones," said Romanova, "Take the weapon, Ivan, and practice until you've exhausted the next quiver."

She gestured with one hand toward the back of the house.

"Mr. Jones and I have business to discuss."

14

IT WAS THE GOATS THAT FINALLY DROVE EDIK BACK INTO THE SHIP. Dola's periodic complaints about never getting to chase birds — which was ridiculous, since the feline familiar didn't need to eat — were bad enough, but when an honest-to-God herd of goats came up onto the lawn, Edik decided he'd had enough.

"Come on," he said, "Let's close it up and wait for Jones to come back."

Dola looked back and forth between the distant singing birds and Edik so fast it sent ripples down his gray fur.

"Now," said Edik, making his point by walking back in himself.

Dola followed a moment later, tail hanging and giving Edik a betrayed look.

Edik closed the hatch, dropped onto the deep, cushioned leather of the nearest passenger seat, crossed his boots at the ankle and stared down at Dola.

"Tell me you're just giving me a hard time. Tell me you don't *really* have some sort of primal urge to go chasing birds."

Dola snickered, tail popping up high where it belonged. "You just looked so thoroughly inconsolable that I had to do something. And once I'd started, well, I had to commit to the bit." He licked a paw and swiped it across his ears. "You understand."

"Thank. God." Three pulses of an exhausted chuckle made their way past his lips. "If you started dropping mice on my boots in the morning, I'd swear—"

"I might still do that. You don't eat enough."

Edik grabbed the armrests and thrust himself to his feet.

"Come on, we might as well get back to those forms." Edik went back to the pilot's chair, where the lingering scent of borscht — made himself from his grandmother's recipe — was a comfort. He called up the ship's phantasmal workspace, instantly producing the forms he needed to fill out yet for Kennedy about his fuel consumption and passenger loads. Faster, smoother, and more precise than the chimerical workspace in his office, the ship's phantasmal workspace made Edik consider, once again, just giving up the storefront and doing all his work from the ship.

"You'd lose business," said Dola in a sing-song voice.

"That's it." Edik spun in the chair to face the grinning cat. "Can you read my mind or what?"

Behind him, the comm pulsed red and toned a deep, cycling hum.

"Better get that," said Dola, tail twitching. "Could be important."

Edik growled and spun to face the comm web. He could have pinched the sparking strand to open the line, but he chose the in-flight option. He tapped his hand on the pad underneath.

The unwelcome sight of Roger North's head materialized above the comm web. Short black hair to match his short black heart. Bushy eyebrows and bloodshot eyes. Heavy jaw, and a nose that some lucky bastard had gotten to break at least once before Edik ever met him.

"What's this I hear about you slandering me, Barshai?"

"Slandering, hell. You're a fare-stealing bastard and you know it."

"'Til you have their money they ain't your fares. I want a formal apology to me and my staff."

"Fuck your apology," said Edik, leaning forward to come eye-to-eye with the illusory form. "I want restitution. Lot of money you cost me."

"Wasn't your money, and you had no right to scare my staff. Or to try to hire away my receptionist."

"Edmund McCutcheon's not *your* receptionist, he's the receptionist of your *shared* office space, which means it's none of your damned business. And your staff needs to know they're working for a fare-stealing bastard."

"That's *it*, Barshai! I challenge you to a duel."

"Fine. I choose swords. I win you give me every penny those Terrans paid you this morning, plus any tips, and McCutcheon verifies the totals. *And* you swear to leave my fares alone."

"I win and you apologize to me and my staff, leave *my* receptionist where he is, and swear to never cause problems for Northbound Tours again."

"Deal. Where and when?"

"The Failed Site, just inside the Barrier. You know it?"

"Of course I know it," laughed Edik. "*I* include it in my tours you cheap bastard."

"Dusk today. And bring a witness. I will."

North had the audacity to cut the connection before Edik could, which irritated him no end.

"Edik," said Dola slowly, "what did North mean, bring a witness?"

"We'll be outside a city proper, so one witness each means—"

"No. I know that. I just mean, why did North choose there? And who does he have in mind for a witness?"

Edik tugged at his Van Dyke, but had no answer. And an unsettled feeling in his stomach made him wish he had one.

15

FROM THE FRONT, CARL WOULD HAVE THOUGHT THAT THE ROMANOVS had left no room behind their gigantic mansion. It had appeared to have been built directly into the side of the mountain.

Turned out that this was and was not the case.

It was the case in the sense that the great, gray mountain did abut the mansion in places. But just there past the rear corner of the house, they'd cut a sweeping stairway into the mountain, leading up. The smell of the lunar rock face was ... metallic, as though it contained more iron than Carl thought it did. Certainly there weren't many local iron mines he'd heard of.

As she led the way up those stairs, Romanova spoke a bit about the history of her family and their decision to relocate to the moon, but honestly Carl didn't pay much attention to this part of the conversation. He was more interested in the precise cuts of the deep stairs. Likely elemental work. Wide enough and deep enough that those guards likely had no trouble riding four abreast up and down, even at speed.

Which meant, conveniently, that a good number of guests could travel both directions without any impediments. The rail on each side shone like gold, but felt like ceramics to the touch.

Three hundred stairs up to the next level, and Romanova never paused in her history lesson through the climb. Blah blah blah, the old country, blah blah blah, new opportunities. The Tsars this and Stalin that and the moon some other thing.

A sniper with a crossbow on almost any one of these steps could take out a partygoer on any one of the nearest six fancy balconies and likely escape into the night before anyone could respond. Which meant they had to have guard posts...

There. And there. Carl could see them because he knew where and how to look. Two grooves in the side of the mountain, just in the right places for armed guards to keep watch without spoiling the view in either direction, either for guests or their hosts.

Place was a fortress. Why did they need a fortress in a place where just getting here was difficult enough?

Carl couldn't keep the question to himself.

"I'm sorry. I have to ask. Why such fortifications?"

"Excuse me?" said Romanova, blinking at him, perhaps surprised that he was not thrilled by the narrative of her personal history.

"You've got guard pods cut into the side of the mountain, which means tunnels as well. I've seen twenty-six armed men on horseback, and their movements make me suspect at least fourteen more that I haven't seen, all just currently on patrol." Carl stopped, feet on two different steps. "Are you expecting an assault today?"

Romanova laughed, a brighter sound than Carl expected.

"Goodness, no." Her hand came to a silver chain at her neck, which had a locket dangling down inside her dress. "None of our enemies would be so brazen as that. We would crush them."

She emphasized their defeat by slapping her knuckles against her palm.

"Then why?"

"Because, Mr. Jones, if we did not keep so many guards on duty at all times, one of our enemies might be foolish enough to *try*."

And with that she turned and continued up the stairs, picking up her narrative as though he hadn't interrupted. Carl caught up with her, wondering just how many guards — no, not guards. Soldiers. How many soldiers the Romanovs and their enemies employed.

That, however, was a question he knew better than to ask.

When they reached the top of the staircase, Romanova finished her monolog with, "And now, we have established ourselves as the most powerful family on Luna. A new world. A new way. But roots as old as the motherland, and those roots give us strength."

But even those words Carl only half heard. Before him was a ... well, it was so grand and sweeping he needed a moment to parse it. A few blinks later, it clicked into place. Rose bushes. Hundreds. Thousands maybe. Reds and whites and pinks and yellows and blues and purples, even black and a cerulean as pure as the eyes of that cat familiar of Barshai's. So fragrant up here that Carl felt as though the very air were a cloud of rose perfume.

He glanced back at the top of the staircase, letting his mind relax enough to look for magic. Sure enough, some sort of enchantment. Likely holding back the fragrance so as not to tip the surprise.

Carl looked back ahead of him. All those huge rose plants were not arranged in neat rows by color or shape of bloom. Instead, they looked to have been arranged into a version of a hedge maze, growing up along trellises two meters tall that followed curving, swirling patterns. Along the outside were arranged wooden benches, some six meters apart and spaced out all the way around the maze.

In the middle, if Carl's eyes didn't deceive him, sat a simple stone bench. But that couldn't be right. No way the Romanovs had anything "simple" in the middle of all that.

"What's the center bench do?"

"Well spotted," Romanova said with approval. "I'm afraid that only those who make it through the maze get the answer to that question, and while I would love to watch you tackle the challenge, we simply don't have time for that today."

"Miss Romanova, why am I here?"

"Before we get to that, I'm afraid I have questions that need answers."

Carl narrowed his eyes. "On the condition that those answers don't infringe on any confidences I am obliged to keep."

"Fair enough," she said with a nod. She gestured to the wooden benches, but when Carl showed no inclination to sit, she remained standing as well. "That champion you faced a few hours ago. Matei Negrescu. Was he sent after you by Alexei Lukyanov or someone else?"

"That's a matter of public record."

"Nonetheless, I'd prefer to hear the answer from your lips."

"Alexei Lukyanov."

"But you didn't sleep with his daughter, did you?"

Surprise question. Romanova probably caught a lot of people off their guard that way, especially in a setting like this. But Carl's training suppressed facial responses faster than she could have guessed.

"That is a matter between Anna Lukyanova and myself, and the answer isn't yours for the asking."

"I don't need the answer anyway," she said with a smile. "Anna did a poor job of hiding her disapproval of her match with my Ivan. No doubt she hired you to pretend to be the great despoiler, counting on your reputation to keep her father from sending the family champion for you."

Romanova sighed. "Impetuous youth. I could have told her that wouldn't work."

I did tell her, thought Carl. He itched to ask questions. To call out her presumptions. But he knew better. Anything he said or did would confirm her suspicions.

So Carl only stared back, face as neutral as he could manage.

"Her choice was excellent. You're handsome enough to be desirable, dangerous enough to be tempting, and have no name or reputation here to recommend you as a husband. Very believable as the sort of man who would claim her virginity and leave her to the aftermath."

Carl clenched his jaw to keep his mouth shut. He could think of several flaws in her logic. Several reasons she should believe exactly what Anna wanted her to believe.

But if he gave voice to any one of them, Romanova would hear the lie.

But he did have one question he couldn't resist asking.

"Isn't Ivan too young to marry? Anna, at least, is of legal age. Ivan's a good four years younger, perhaps five."

"Six, actually," Romanova said, humor in her icy blue eyes. "As of next week when Anna turns twenty. But Ivan is old enough to wed here on Luna, and when he does, he will be considered a full adult, ready to run the business I plan to give him as a wedding gift. A gift that, thanks to you, Anna will not get to enjoy with him."

Carl could feel Romanova's eyes bore into him, straining to find the answers she sought. Not so certain as she sounded, perhaps?

"You're good," she said at last. "Most men would have tipped something by now. Very well, let's move on to another subject."

"As you like, but I should say that I thought we would discuss business today, and I've taken a fair amount of time and expense to put myself at your disposal."

"Oh, that," she said with a wave of dismissal. "If we come to no arrangement, I will compensate you for your time and costs." She clasped her hands. "Now then. You have made yourself an enemy of the Lukyanov family today. And I am given to understand that you enjoy spending time in Kennedy, is that correct?"

"I would say it's my favorite spaceport, but not necessarily my favorite city."

"You *are* a cagey one," Romanova said with a smile that made her look even younger. "Very well, for my purposes I will suppose that you like Kennedy well enough to desire to return there with some frequency. Fair to say?"

"For the sake of argument," he conceded.

"Excellent. Then let us get to my proposal." She smoothed her dress and stood taller. "I wish you to challenge Alexie Lukyanov to a duel for the expressed purpose of freeing his daughter to marry whomever she wishes. Yourself, should you choose to put yourself forward as a suitor."

"I can't duel as your champion for that end point. Not even up here. There has to be personal cause, either legal or moral or, well, personal."

"I don't mean that you should stand champion for me. I wish you to do this representing yourself."

"Doesn't work that way," said Carl with a shake of his head and a canceling wave of his hands. "You can only hire a champion to represent *you*, your family or your businesses. Things like that. You can't hire me to—"

"I won't be hiring you. Officially. I want to hire you *un*officially."

A clenching muscle deep in Carl's gut urged him to run back down those stairs.

He forced his feet to keep him where he stood.

"I don't think—"

"Then don't think," Romanova said, steel in her voice. "Listen. I own a tour agency in Kennedy that books vacations. The profit margins are excellent, the managers handle the business well and honorably, and every year the liners offer free trips that you could enjoy. You'd make a solid living without risking your life, and you could travel about as much as you could want to, for free."

She pressed her hands together, the palms flat against each other.

"I will arrange to transfer that business to you through shell companies. No one knows I own it now, almost no one could prove it, and certainly no one will connect your ownership of it to me. And all you have to do to get it is kill Alexei Lukyanov in a legal, witnessed duel."

She stepped closer. Her breath smelled of spearmint.

"Make the duel about Anna. Make whatever excuse you want. But kill Alexei Lukyanov for me, and I will make you a wealthy man."

16

Edik paced back and forth the length of the main passenger cabin, while Dola lounged on a center seat, eyes swiveling to watch under the golden light shining down from the cabin-long firebird tail feather mural above.

The hatch was open again. Fresher air filling the cabin with the smell of grass.

"Where is he?" said Edik for the sixteenth time.

"Shall I investigate?" asked Dola, for the first.

Edik stopped, spun on his heels, and faced the sprawling familiar.

"Do you want to?"

"Depends," said Dola through a yawn. "How well do you think the Romanovs would take your familiar prowling around their grounds without an invitation? I mean, yes, I can hide myself from normal vision, but if they have a magician, or if Jones spots me—"

"I get the point."

"I mean, I'll do it. If you want. Anything to get away from your pacing. Can't promise I won't get sidetracked by chasing a bird or two—"

Edik chuckled out of habit and dropped into one of the chairs, his scabbard sliding easily under the armrest and out of the way. But that nervous edge still keened along his spine. His fingers drummed on the armrests. His boot heels bounced off the red carpeting. His eyes kept glancing toward the hatch.

"There are more forms in need of—"

"How much longer can he need? We're bleeding sunlight here."

"I could go inquire of a servant. Surely that wouldn't violate any protocols." Dola's whiskers twitched. "In their minds, I'm basically a servant myself."

"I see no reason to compound the errors in their thinking," snapped Edik.

He drew a deep breath and pressed the heels of his hands against his eyes.

"I'm sorry. I didn't mean—"

"Nothing to apologize for," said Dola, making a half-hearted effort at cleaning a hind leg. "Me, Nixia, the others. We understand. Your view isn't in fashion among you modern wizards—"

"Magicians." Edik's fingers drummed along the armrests again.

"Magi, sorcerers, thaumaturgists. Call yourselves medicine men for all the difference it makes to us. Actions. Decisions. These are what matter to us."

Something about the simple, matter of fact tone cut through the haze in Edik's mind. He looked over at Dola, now busy cleaning between the toes of a forepaw.

"What are you telling me?"

"Nothing you don't already know. If you'd stop to think about it."

"No. Wait."

Edik held his tongue until Dola looked up, but the feline spirit was in no hurry to finish with that paw. How many times had he witnessed Dola talking to another familiar, in words that only they could understand? Conversations Dola declined to explain or discuss later?

Conjuring a familiar wasn't like a normal spirit binding. Yes, it involved calling between the worlds, but it was an open call. It sought a spirit compatible with the goals and personality of the magician.

And the answering spirit gained form in this world through the alchemy involved in its binding.

Dola was, quite literally, part of Edik. But part of that familiar was something unique and independent, and at times, thoroughly alien, despite its casual demeanor.

Finally, Dola finished that paw and looked up, an inscrutable expression in those cerulean eyes.

"Are you telling me that the spirits we call and bind—"

"I'm telling you that the way you wizards see and deal with spirits changes over the centuries, and varies from culture to culture. *You*, Edik, treat us as allies. You care. To others, we are mere tools."

Edik sat up straight. Leaned forward.

"That's not all you mean. I can hear it in your tone. See that smile hiding in your eyes. What are you telling me?"

"Let's get the hell out of here," said Jones, stepping inside. Surprise brought Edik to his feet.

"I'll get her prepped," said Dola, swishing off through the closed door to the bridge.

Edik looked back and forth between the bridge door and Jones, who even now was managing to trigger the hatch door to close. Which only an employee of Firebird Travel — that is, Edik or one of his spirits — should have been able to do.

"Come on," said Jones. "The faster I'm airborne the happier I'll be."

Edik's appointment just inside the Kennedy Barrier jolted back into his mind.

"Right," he said, heading for the bridge, Jones on his heels. Edik slipped into the pilot's seat, and Nixia already waited for him, floating in the air above his workstation, her yellow swirls of skin flushed orange with excitement. She called up the phantasmal workstation for him.

"Are we going straight to the Failed Site?" she said.

"Failed site?" echoed Jones.

"No, back to Kennedy first," said Edik, and Nixia dissolved, off to convey orders. Edik checked his readouts. The *Third Son* was airborne and moving before he could spin to address Jones. "You said you had an appointment later. I hope it's in Kennedy."

"No," said Jones, reaching for a seatbelt in the bridge's secondary chair, but his hands didn't find one. There wasn't one on this chair, any more than on the pilot's chair. Edik had never needed them. Jones continued, "No, I said I *might*. I had to be ready in case they offered me a job."

"They didn't?"

"They did, but ... they didn't. It's hard to explain."

"Probably something sick and twisted," said Edik, spinning around to check his ship's status by poking sections of the tiny illusory image of his ship. Each prodded section reported a healthy green color. "What would you expect from a title-less woman who lives like a *knyazhna*."

"Yazh-na?"

"*Knyazhna*. Like a princess or a duchess." Edik called up reports from the local ports. Petrograd was pulling in heavy traffic, and there was a report of the Terran Navy shooting at something an hour ago, but clear skies prevailed now. In mocking tones, he said, "Seeking a rebirth of glory."

"You're just bitter," said Dola in words that only Edik could understand, "that they won't let you into the house."

Edik whirled on Dola and said, in plain English, "Well it's just plain rude."

"Excluding someone from the conversation?" said Jones. "Yeah, I agree."

"It was nothing," said Edik.

"Anyway, Kennedy's fine with me. Oh, and I've got confirmation on my zephyrpad that the Romanovs are paying for my flight today, and your time."

A zephyrpad. Strictly a magician's tool, but Edik hadn't heard of anyone under Journeyman grade using one. He only used memopads himself. Word was an Initiate couldn't get full use of them. And Jones was no Journeyman.

Still...

"How did you close the hatch?" asked Edik, and was gratified to hear a sharp intake of breath from Jones. Still, Edik scrolled through reports of traffic in the air around Kennedy, but listened intently, when he asked, "I was pretty sure only I and my bound spirits could close that hatch."

"There's a loose spot in the spell," said Jones, a sigh in his voice. "It's small, but there, if you know how to look for it."

"Handy talent."

"From time to time." Jones' tone closed up again. In Edik's opinion, the man had slipped up when he closed the hatch in his haste to leave, and was willing to talk about that, but Edik had gotten all he was going to get right now.

Fares were like that from time to time. They'd let slip about problems in their love life, or their family, or their businesses. Next thing Edik would know, they'd rambled on about private things for a minute, or five, or thirty. Until all of a sudden they'd realize what they were doing, then *slam*. Close up like they'd never said a word.

There were tricks for keeping the information tap flowing, but once that *slam* came, any of them would have come across as an intrusion.

But handled right, sometimes, they'd get going again. And those little insights, and the trust that surrounded them, had helped Edik gain repeat business and steady customers.

So Edik offered something personal in return. Nothing to match, of course, but a little something.

"After I drop you off, I have to head to the Failed Site. I've got a duel coming at dusk with a fare-stealing bastard who owes me restitution."

"Sounds fierce."

Edik glanced back at Jones, who stared away out the bridge viewer. Edik turned his eyes back to reports he didn't need to read.

"Could use a witness, if you aren't doing anything."

"Witness or a second?"

From staring into the distance to a direct, business tone in a single question.

"Just a witness. No seconds for the duel. Can't say there won't be trouble, though. I don't trust the guy at all."

Nothing for a moment, and that moment stretched. Edik was just about to look back again when Jones spoke.

"Yeah. I'll witness for you."

17

THE MADRONE WOOD OF THE LOWER HALLS CREAKED THIS TIME OF YEAR.
Anna had never mastered the trick of keeping her weight distributed
the way her sister Rada had. But she had learned that if she stayed to
the kitchen side of the hall, and avoided bumping the gilt frames of
the huge old still lifes, she kept the creaking to a minimum.

And ever since Father had paid for the diffuse, sourceless lighting
that had become so fashionable, the whole house was lit both day
and night. Slipping unseen anywhere had become next to impossible,
so unheard was her best bet.

Matei's funeral was in an hour. The thought of that brought tears
to her eyes even now, even when she needed her focus on every step.
Poor Matei. He had loved her. She had seen it in his eyes, heard it in
her tone. The foolish love of a hopeless romantic. Father would no
sooner have allowed her to marry Matei than that champion, Carl.

Not that Anna wished to marry any of them.

Still, Matei had loved her. And she had gotten him killed through
her arrogance. Through her belief that Father would have accepted a
first-blood duel as satisfying honor. That he would not have pushed
for death.

Her heart pounded in her chest now, and her breaths were

ragged. That was no good. If any of the servants stepped into the hall right now, a glance would tell them she was up to something.

She couldn't afford that. She was a Lukyanova. She was allowed to feel fear, but none must ever see it.

Especially now, when she wasn't even dressed for Matei's funeral. Father would expect her to wear that black lace and chiffon dress, the one that covered her from high on her neck to the ends of her wrists and ended just at her ankles. He would expect to see her blonde hair bound back in a black lace hair net, and to see an onyx bracelet of mourning on her left wrist.

Anna did wear the bracelet. It was the least she could do for poor Matei. And given a choice, she would have been wearing black, but of that color she had only the one article of clothing. Instead she wore tan riding pants and boots, and a blue linen shirt enchanted to withstand the elements well and keep her warm, as well as setting off her eyes.

Nothing like mourning clothes, but Anna could not afford to waste Matei's sacrifice by attending his funeral. Father would see the list she'd written for him — the word "alchemy" written in each numbered entry of the ten item list — and would not wait for privacy before unleashing his tantrum.

Punishment would follow. And when that was done, he would dispose of her once and for all. Perhaps marry her to a lesser family possessed of some money.

Perhaps worse.

She had no intention of waiting around to find out.

But first she needed to calm herself, or not even the dullest maid would believe she was going for a ride before the funeral. So she paused where she stood, and flared her nose in a deep breath.

The hall smelled of beeswax, a clever trick on the part of whoever provided the light. Persistent spells like this one required alchemical preservation, especially spells with switchable qualities like dimming or extinguishing the light. Mixing beeswax with the preservation oil would provide the subtle suggestion of candlelight.

Anna would remember that, if she ever needed to blend her own.

She could smell the oils of the nearest painting — the hard curves of river near Kivach Falls in Russia — and the aged cotton of its canvas. But underneath that she detected acidic traces of preservation oil at the corners of the gilt frame, keeping the painting than deteriorating further than it had already.

Her stomach rumbled. One of these smells — the beeswax? — reminded her that she had skipped lunch and eaten nothing since the goat cheese and chicken eggs of breakfast.

No time for that now. But her heart rate was back under control. Breathing too.

Anna straightened her posture and hastened her steps along the madrone wood floor.

She made it out the door, waved in passing to the gardeners who were trimming the laurel hedges of the labyrinth. The stables were straight ahead of her, and off to her left was a patio area for entertaining. Smooth reddish stonework, with wrought iron chairs and tables, forged at considerable expense. The pools and fountains were beyond that.

Inside the stable, heavy old Ulik, the averner, looked up from casting a spell to seal the split hoof of Father's favorite palomino, Hurricane. The hay smell was everywhere, and horse, but Ulik always managed to keep the manure smell at bay.

"Hardly time to ride, is there, Miss?" he said. "Can't be an hour 'til that funeral. Better get changed."

"I have time," she said, stepping past him and straight to her roan gelding, Whisper. "I just need a few minutes to clear my head."

"Don't take him running." Ulik stood, wiping his hands. "Didn't think you'd ride the next couple days, so I made sure he stretched his legs good."

"Just a few minutes," she said, throwing her brown saddle over Whisper's back, and tying it with the speed and skill of years of practice. "All the stands between me and madness. I promise you."

Ulik looked as though he had a mind to argue, but finally said, "All right then. But it better be just a few minutes. And I'll make sure he gets rubbed down good, but you make sure you come back later this evening and brush him out anyway."

Anna waited until Ulik threw open the gate to say, "I promise. If I run him hard for even a second, I'll be right back here tonight to brush him out. I just want to trot around a little."

And then Whisper walked her out of the stable and turned away from the house as though he'd read her mind. "Good boy," she whispered," and as she promised, she held him back to a gentle trot, out toward the spruce grove, trying for all the world to look as though the path through the spruces was her goal.

And not the landing field before it, where her father's red airship sat idle.

Anna's heart was pounding again, and Whisper tried to speed up, feeling her urgency. But Anna held him back. Bad enough she wouldn't be here later to brush him down. Overworking him would have been downright criminal.

And Anna had done enough damage for one day.

Instead she held him to a slow trot, out around the landing field until the airship lay between her and the stable. The airship, which father named *Morning's Glory*, did not follow the current avian trend in airship design. Instead it looked like a great red disc, with three articulated legs to land on, and a bubble cockpit up top with enough seating for four.

Once Anna felt certain she was unobserved, she quickly dismounted and tied Whisper to a branch of the nearest spruce. Then she returned to the airship and tapped the nearest leg with a tiny silver disc that — she hoped — Father forgot he gave her.

It had been a small incident. A party at the Pajari house three years ago, the first party Anna was to attend alone, apart, of course, from an attending servant. Father gave her a copy of the airship passkey in case Garrick gave in to his weakness and overindulged while waiting with the other servants.

Anna had "forgotten" to return the passkey, and Father appeared not to notice.

He would notice now.

When she touched the ship's leg with her passkey, a panel above her opened, and a ladder slid straight down. Anna grabbed the rungs, and the ladder retreated, pulling her up inside the silver cockpit. Four plush seats, including the pilot's station. A cooler in the center of the floor, probably filled with water, cheeses and beer even now.

Anna didn't worry about the cooler. She didn't have time. Father might be looking for her right now. When he saw the airship missing, he would know. He would understand.

He would come after her.

But he would expect her to go to her friends. Or to King, with its great department of Alchemy at the University.

But he would never look for her in so mundane a place as Kennedy.

Anna looked over the panel at the flight stick and comm pad. Physical, not chimerical or phantasmal. Her pulse pounded in her ears as she cast her mind back, remembering what she could from a handful of lessons and a single time at the controls. She grabbed the flight stick and gave it a twist to power up the airship.

Anna gave a shaky laugh when the chimerical display opened up. She remembered! Not much to the display, at least not that she understood. But she could tell the airship had enough fuel to feed the kinetic spells that powered the ship for five hours, which should get her to Kennedy. In the air to her right, above the panel, an air map of Luna, with special destinations marked.

She sped past the family Barrier and into the slowly darkening sky.

18

In his time serving Earth, Carl had seen more places than he could count. Some eighty three countries on the home world, and over a hundred-fifty cities. Ten more cities on Mars, only the one on Venus (if he could even call Gilgamesh a city), but all thirty-eight cities here on Luna.

But Carl had never seen anything like the Failed Site.

First of all, that name. When Barshai had first mentioned in while trying to ask for a hand without trying to hire a champion, Carl had assumed that "Failed Site" was a nickname. Something the locals called an embarrassment.

Like that section of San Francisco, just off of Mission, that had yet to get rebuilt. Every single one of the buildings were absolute wrecks. Some burnt out, others crushed, and others just eerily empty and distant in a way that made people fear to get too close to them. The locals called that area "the Ruins." But it wasn't a name you'd find on a map.

The Failed Site had a placard: "The Failed Site. Here lie the remains of the first, shortsighted attempt to establish a human presence on the moon. Two hundred died. Their buildings have been taken down. Their spells unwoven. Let none repeat their errors, but let none forget them." And underneath were the names of all two hundred of the first settlers including, Carl noted, two MaTs and a Th.D.

How could two Magisters and a Hierophant have gone so very wrong? And if they had, why build Kennedy so close by? The Failed Site was inside Kennedy's Barrier, only fifteen minutes by air from the port city itself.

"What happened?" asked Carl, looking behind him at Barshai, who paced back and forth in front of his ship's hatch. Sword already naked in his hand, which made Carl want to cluck his tongue.

"What?" said Barshai.

"He means to the first settlers," said ... Dola. Carl was sure the familiar's name was Dola. "He wants to know what happened."

"Take the to—" Barshai stopped pacing and wiped his face with his free hand. Already sweating. In Carl's experience, that wasn't a good sign. "Sorry. Look out there and tell me what you see."

Carl looked out over a field some two hundred acres square. To the right were a row of two hundred graves, but Carl had a feeling that wasn't the answer.

But the ground was flat. Level. All gray rock and sand, with a slight greenish hint.

Greenish hint?

"It's the color, isn't it?"

"Now smell."

"Alkaline. Bay leaves. And is that ginger?"

"Yes," said Dola.

"They didn't come up with the Barrier right away," said Barshai, his baritone falling into what had to be his tour guide voice. "The first settlers tried to change the land itself to support us. A Hierophant and two Magisters, all sure they'd figured out the keys to sustaining human life in an unfriendly environment. They were wrong, and they took another hundred ninety-seven people down with them."

"The Barrier works better though?"

"You've seen it. Just like Earth, here inside the Barrier. Or close enough anyway. If you don't mind your sky pale green and your air smelling just a little bit like licorice."

Carl smacked his palm. "That's what it is! I've never been able to put my finger on it."

"You get used to it."

"Over on Mars the sky is blue and the air tastes just like it does around the Mediterranean. But the locals are slowly turning red. Seen anything like that here on the moon?"

Barshai's eyes tracked something in the sky. Carl followed his glance up and saw an airship like a great sparrow in flight.

Barshai sheathed his sword. Not *entirely* gauche then.

"That's the guy?" said Carl.

"Roger North. Calls his ship the *Sparrow*. Have you ever heard anything more boring?"

Carl shrugged. He'd ridden on more than his share of ships, and the way they got their names made no sense to him at all. "No mistaking it, at least. Maybe it's a professional thing."

Barshai gave Carl a look that suggested that after the coming duel finished, he would be more than happy to part Carl's head from the shoulders beneath it.

"So that's a no then," said Carl.

The cat snickered.

"No," said Barshai, but then his attention was entirely on the landing airship.

A swoop and flutter of wings, an extension of claws, and the *Sparrow* alighted next to the *Third Son*, a name that must have made sense to Barshai, though Carl couldn't make heads or tails of it. Was it some kind of fairy tale thing? Or did he have two older brothers?

Part of the bird's belly opened like a door, and out stepped a man who'd seen plenty of fights in his day, and won more than he lost. Carl could see it in every part of him. Big arms, big barrel chest, sure, easy steps. Blocky jaw, craggy forehead and twice, no, thrice broken nose. Short scruffy black hair and beard. Skin weathered like he flew with the hatch open. He wore one of those mock uniforms, loved by civilians who didn't have the guts to serve. Tight cut and navy blue, with gold clusters at the collar intended to be mistaken for rank, and his surname over his heart in block letters. Military-style black boots that came halfway up his calf.

And he smelled like he'd been doing wind sprints, then bathed in olive oil.

"You brought a champion?" The voice matched the face. Rough. "Thought you were man enough to fight for yourself."

"He's my witness," said Barshai, fingers already clenching and relaxing like he wanted his sword.

"Well meet mine," said North. "Oh, wait, you've already met."

Out came a kid who looked like he should have been in college. Neat, erect posture, perfect hygiene, close-cropped curls and skin almost as dark as Carl's own. Crisp shirt and pants, white and black respectively, and a dark blue tie that made Carl think he needed more of that color in his own wardrobe.

The guy looked like Carl's kid brother Duane, who was an attorney somewhere along the Oakland-Berkeley border.

"Edmund," said Barshai in a friendly tone, extending a hand to shake, "good, a witness I can trust."

"Captain Barshai." Edmund said the name like a greeting while they shook hands, then got inquisitive. "Is it true that my future employment hangs in the balance of this duel?"

Carl spoke before anyone else could. "They can commit themselves to things they will or won't do, but your choices are your own. If anyone wishes to dispute that, then I'd be happy to explain to them the error of their ways."

Damn, this Edmund looked like Duane.

"He swore that if he lost," said North, "he'd leave my receptionist right where he was."

"Which means," said Carl in a silencing tone, "that if he loses, Barshai here cannot offer you a job while you work for ... North is it?"

"Technically I work for the owner of the office building."

"Doesn't matter. Their agreement can't bind you from quitting your job, nor from applying for a job with Barshai."

"*He can't hire him!*" yelled North.

"You have to beat me first," said Barshai.

Both men had their hands on their sword hilts. Barshai had a saber, and North something like a cutlass. More affectation than effective choice, in Carl's opinion, but that would come down to the men fighting the duel.

"Enough," said Carl. "Are you men here to duel or brawl?" As they got hold of themselves, Carl stepped up to Edmund. "Technically, if they agreed to it in advance, Barshai could be made to refuse you employment."

"That wasn't the deal," said Barshai.

"Yes it was," said North.

"Dola!"

The cat jumped down from the hatch, trotted over to stand between Barshai and North, but faced Carl. Dola conjured images of two faces, Barshai's and North's, and North's looked a little less ... formed. Probably present over a comm.

"Fine," said the miniature Barshai. "I choose swords. I win you give me every penny those Terrans paid you this morning, plus any tips, and McCutcheon verifies the totals. *And* you swear to leave my fares alone."

"I win and you apologize to me and my staff," responded the miniature North, "leave *my* receptionist where he is, and swear to never cause problems for Northbound Tours again."

Carl nodded, then turned to Edmund. "If North wins and you remain in your current post, Barshai cannot hire you away nor offer you any further negotiation or terms. But if you quit, he can give you a job, under terms you've already discussed or new ones."

"Don't try to lawyer me," barked North, stepping toward Carl.

Carl let his eyes cool to dueling levels and placed his hand on the hilt of his sword.

"You disputing my interpretation?"

North stopped moving. His hand fell away from his cutlass.

"You want a judge," said Carl, "then hire a judge. But I don't see one, that makes me the closest thing you've got. I've heard the words as recorded by a familiar, and that's good enough for me."

Carl eased his hand away from his own sword, and folded his arms over his chest.

"Now, are you two going to duel or not? Because I've had a long day and my patience is wearing *thin*."

19

DUSK SETTLED AROUND THE GREENISH, LEVEL TERRAIN OF THE FAILED Site like the sheet thrown over a corpse. If the corpse had an alkaline smell, with hints of ginger and bay leaves. The *Third Son* and the *Sparrow* both had external lamps that drove away the growing gloom and gave Edik — and probably North — enough light to see by. At least, enough light for the duel.

Jones made them stand seven paces apart, as though he were officiating, but it didn't matter to Edik. Five paces, seven paces, a hundred paces. Soon enough they'd be blade to blade, and then, oh yes, and then.

Eagerness sang through Edik's veins. His heart kept a steady march but his breaths came deep and full. He could feel the smile in his eyes as he looked across the distance at North.

A cutlass. Who carries a cutlass in this day and age? Clearly the man aspired to be a pirate, which suited his fare-stealing nature.

"*En—*" started North, but Jones interrupted.

"*Wait.*" He looked back and forth between Edik and North. Maybe making sure he had their attention, or maybe just pausing for dramatic effect. Tough to tell with this one. When he continued, he said, "Is this to first blood? First to yield? Don't tell me it's to the death."

Edik and North looked at one another. He was eager enough for North's death, and he was sure North was eager for his.

"Please," said Edmund. "Not to the death. Please."

Edik looked away. North cleared his throat, probably ready to tell them the ways of Luna. But Jones, damn it, spoke first again.

"Bad news, boys, since both your witnesses agree you're not dueling to the death, you're not."

"That's our choice," said Edik.

"If you had a crowd, sure." Jones was grinning now. "But it's just the two of us. Legally speaking, familiars don't count. Not for this. So if you two decide this is to the death, Edmund and I are going to take a walk. Do some sightseeing while there's still a little light."

"You said you'd witness!" yelled North at Edmund.

"Not killing," said Edmund, sounding a little sick. "You never said anything about killing."

"So choose," said Jones, his grin almost smug now. "First blood, first to yield … or *murder*."

Just the word made Edmund shudder.

"Fine," growled North. "Might as well be first blood then. Agreed, you miserable slandering sky rat?"

"Agreed, you vomitus fare-stealing, stinking bastard."

"*En garde*," said North, and charged, cutlass swinging.

Edik parried with a side step, but North was past him before he could counter. Edik closed, point leading, just as happy to cut North's arm and win as he would have been to scar the bastard's cheek.

All right, *almost* as happy to just win.

But despite the unusual choice of a cutlass, North was quick to parry with circular swipes that functioned almost as ripostes, for purposes of just scoring a hit. Edik had to retreat as fast as he advanced, and North kept moving with him.

Edik regained the advantage with a feint-thrust combination that got North's blade out of line. Made him jump backward to avoid the hit. Edik followed hard, thrusting and cutting. North kept backpedaling.

Edik had him on the run now, but Edik had been out here many times. Knew where the ground had breaks. He kept advancing, pushed North back and back. Steering him.

Then North's boot caught a loose rock.

Down he went.

A high, distant Doppler sound. A flash of light at the Barrier, high up to Edik's right. Drew his eyes.

A huge red disc airship came down at unsafe speeds.

Edik thrust again without looking, but North had already rolled to his feet. Recovered his balance. Came back on the attack. Slashing, slashing. No target in particular, just a slashing blade, cutting back and forth and determined to hit something.

And North swung the cutlass with enough force that Edik's parries got his saber knocked back at him.

On the next incoming swing — likely aimed at his head — Edik parried up with all the force he could muster, forcing North's sword too high.

Edik dove, tucking into a roll that carried him to North's unprotected back.

Edik came up spinning, thrusting as soon as his feet were under him.

Too late. North had jumped forward. Edik charged. Lunged...

The red disc airship crashed, rocking the ground and throwing Edik's aim off.

He cut the threads of North's uniform at the rib cage, but failed to draw blood.

Jones and Edmund were on their feet, and Dola between them. Everyone staring at the red airship, and Edik was shocked to realize that he was too. Someone had to be flying it, and that someone needed help.

Thoughts of North and the duel flew out of Edik's head. That was a pilot in trouble, and humanitarian aid came first.

North cut the back of Edik's wrist with his cutlass.

"I win," he said, but Edik barely heard him. Too busy rushing forward, Jones hard on his heels and Dola already ahead of them. Even Edmund was trying to keep up.

The red disc had a bubble top, and the safety foam had triggered. Marvelous stuff. Purely alchemical product. Only the sensor was magic. When the sensor tripped that a crash was immanent, the beakers shattered and stasis safety foam flooded the air.

They might have to dig the pilot out, but the man was likely alive and well in there. Held in a supportive cushion that dispersed the energy of the crash outward from the cabin.

Which meant the poor man's airship had been trashed. Part of the disc had chipped away a chunk of the rock of the Failed Site, but most of the ship had shattered. Only the inner lining of the cockpit was really still intact, and that had more to do with the safety foam than the enchantments in the airship's ceramics.

At least it wasn't an elemental-driven model. Then the pilot would have been responsible for anything the elementals did before shifting back to their own plane of existence.

Not that there was much havoc to cause here. The Failed Site had long since passed its days of havoc.

By the time Edik and Jones got to the bubble, Dola already had it open, paws on the foam, preparing it for the next step in freeing the pilot. They wouldn't have to dig after all.

Jones had his sword out now. Was that a *DeGarmo*? Even in the fading light Edik couldn't miss that maker's mark — an elaborate capital *D* with a tiny *e* in the upper right hand corner.

Not the time. Jones had taken up position on the opposite side from Edik, pommel ready to strike. Edik, his saber still in his hand, shifted his grip to do likewise.

Edik counted down from three and they struck together. Thanks to Dola's preparations, the foam cracked in a spider web pattern, then began to dissolve. The four, well-padded silver seats within remained intact, and Edik realized immediately he had miscast the pilot as a man.

She was a woman all right. Young, maybe not even Edmund's age.

blonde and remarkably beautiful of face and figure. Dressed to ride horses, not fly airships.

Jones' jaw dropped, and Edik's assumption about why vanished a moment later when Jones spoke.

"Anna?"

20

WHAT WAS ANNA LUKYANOVA DOING HERE?

The possibilities were too many for Carl to parse quickly. If he were not looking at her right now, he would never have believed she was here. True, on some level, he expected a message. Some sort of apology for the death duel that she had promised would merely be the satisfaction of honor. First blood or first to yield, at the most.

But he never expected her to come herself to apologize. Certainly not without an escort. Or without a pilot which she — obviously — desperately needed.

No. She shouldn't be here. Not at the Failed Site, not anywhere this close to Kennedy. At dusk. In an airship she ... must have stolen from her father.

Carl pressed the palm of his free hand against his forehead and closed his eyes. His sword hand sheathed his blade. She was running away like a spoiled child. Of course. How could he not have seen that immediately?

"Hello, Carl," she said. Effort in her voice suggested that the stasis foam had made her sluggish. Possibly left her feeling a touch bruised and battered, even though the foam kept her from any real harm. She must have been having trouble getting up.

"You two, ah, *know* each other?" said the leering voice of North from the other side of the crashed airship.

Anna said nothing.

"You could say that," said Carl with a sigh, dropping his hands to his sword belt. "Anna Lukyanova, may I present Captains Edik Barshai and Roger North."

Before Carl could finish the introductions with Barshai's familiar, the man cut him off.

"*I'm* a captain. North only flies an airship. He's a skipper at best."

"I'm every bit the captain you are. Take your false airs and shove them up your—"

"*The familiar,*" Carl continued loudly, "is Barshai's, and goes by Dola."

"Well," started Anna, but North cut her off.

"Doesn't matter what you call me anyway, sky rat, we both know I won. You owe me—"

"*You cheated!*" roared Barshai, and both men drew their swords again, circling each other in the growing night.

Apparently their concern for the crash-landed pilot went no further than their hatred for one another.

Carl held out a hand and helped Anna to her feet. He could see a lot of emotion in her pale blue eyes, and the onyx mourning bracelet didn't exactly match her riding habit.

"Mr. Jones!" yelled Edmund nervously, and a moment later the clash of steel rang out.

"Excuse me," Carl said to Anna, who was nodding *of course* as Carl turned and leapt down to stand between the fighting men, drawing his sword as he did.

"That's *it*," he barked. "I've had it with the two of you. We have an actual emergency to deal with and you two are fighting like children."

"Children rarely try to kill each other," observed the cat in a philosophical voice.

"Well I'm calling for an end to it. Right here. Right now. Your duel ended in a draw this evening and if you want another you have to wait..." — were they close enough to Kennedy to assume that city's rules? They were still inside the Barrier. Close enough — "three days to duel again."

"I already won," said North, pointing at Barshai's left hand. The sunlight had faded, but this close to the giant wall of dark yellow light that was the Barrier, Carl could make out a trickling line on the back of Barshai's hand.

"You cut me during a halt," argued Barshai. "We were interrupted by this woman's crashing ship!"

"No one called a halt," said North. "The cut counts."

"Edmund," said Carl.

"Here," came the response from behind him. It seemed at least one of them was helping Anna out of the wreckage of her ship. And from the weight Carl had felt when pulling her up, she would need help for some time yet.

"Did you witness North cut Barshai on the hand?"

"No, sir. All my attention was on Miss Lukyanova's crashing ship."

"That's where my attention was too. I didn't see any cut either."

"*I cut him! I won!*"

"The cut was not witnessed, not even by the witness you provided. Barshai might have cut himself when the ground shook as the ship crashed. Or maybe he cut himself on a shard of hull ceramics before we freed Anna Lukyanova from the safety foam. As the closest thing to a judge present, I adjudicate that the duel is inconclusive. You'll have to have your rematch in three days."

North unleashed a torrent of invective in general, then spent a flurry at Barshai. But when he turned his words to Carl, Carl raised his sword.

"I would remind you," he said in a quiet voice, "that I am under no obligation to wait three days to duel you. And I tire of your whining. Insult me at your peril."

"He'll kill you," said Anna, closer behind Carl than he expected. Her words came out heavy. "Carl's a master duelist. He probably wouldn't even break a sweat."

North thrust his cutlass back into its scabbard with so much force he staggered back a half-step. Barshai laughed, but when Carl looked at him sideways, Barshai raised his free hand in a halting gesture and sheathed his own saber.

Carl nodded and put his rapier away, then turned to see Anna leaning on Edmund, who studiously kept his supporting hand on her shoulder. Polite, but it wouldn't take enough of her weight.

"Allow me," said Carl, taking Edmund's place and putting his arm around her waist while she hung onto his shoulder. "All right. Your dueling is done for the night, and this woman should see a doctor before she gets to her hotel or wherever—"

"What's that?" Edmund's voice, curious and a little afraid, and so much like Duane that Carl promised himself to visit Oakland again soon.

Carl turned the direction Edmund was pointing, and saw something moving in the gash created by the airship's crash. Down in the crevasse. Slow, thick movements of slow thick limbs.

And nothing about the creature looked human.

21

EDIK ALMOST DIDN'T TURN AND LOOK AT WHATEVER EDMUND WAS pointing at. He was still staring down North. North looked ready to chew through his cutlass at being denied his cheating attempt to win, and Edik didn't want to wait Jones' three days for satisfaction.

If only because Edik didn't want to wait three days for the money. And that cut on the back of his hand might have been shallow, but it itched and bled.

Besides. Edik had been to the Failed Site, and was used the seeing spirits flit about, especially just after the sun had set. He told his tour groups that those were the spirits of the two hundred who died, returning to patrol the site of their demise and ensure that no one ever repeated their mistakes.

But Edik knew better. The dead did not return to haunt us, or help us. The dead moved on to whatever came next. Whatever spirits he saw out here among the greenish rocks and the alkaline smells were just some sort of local phenomenon. The lunar equivalent of fae, perhaps, or free elementals. Something along those lines.

Still, Edmund didn't have any aura of power that even an Initiate carried with him, which made him unlikely to spot spirits. Though stranger things had happened.

Jones, though. Jones did not seem given to fits of nervousness, and Jones let Edmund take over supporting Lukyanova. And given that neither Jones nor Lukyanova had denied North's guess that they were lovers, that was odd behavior.

Edik knew that if he was sleeping with a beautiful woman a decade his junior, and that woman needed support, he would have been damned before he would have left her in another guy's arms.

But Jones had done that, and taken a step toward the crash, hand on his sword hilt.

Edik wanted to look. But could he trust North not to rush him while Jones was distracted?

"Edik," said Dola from over near Jones, "you need to see this."

"Don't do anything stupid," Edik warned North. He even bit down against adding, "though I realize it's impossible for you to do anything else."

Hand on his own hilt he moved to stand over by Jones, passing Lukyanova who was struggling with Edmund, apparently eager for a closer look herself.

When Edik reached Jones and Dola, he started to say, "What have we..."

But then he saw for himself.

Down in the crevasse carved by the crashing airship, maybe fifteen meters away, he could see movement. Edik blinked, trying to parse the images his eyes were sending. Tripod. No. Snake? Lizard? No. Whatever it was glowed, faintly, just enough yellowish-green surrounding it to make its shape discernible against the darkening night around it.

Three legs. Thick as Edik's thigh. All three coming down from a central trunk, as broad at the base as maybe as his own shoulders, but tapering a meter up from there to a rounded point about the width of his fist.

Looked like an odd shape of glowing rock, except it moved. The three legs moved slowly, inching their way out of the crevasse. And the tip, the final third or so, dipped forward and pointed at Dola, then Jones, then Edik.

The tip trembled. Two round spots maybe twenty centimeters from the tip shivered, then glowed the same shade of dark yellow as the Barrier.

"It's alive," said Jones.

"Obviously," said Dola.

"But what is it?" said Edik.

He heard movement behind him. Steps. The back of his neck itched. One of the three people moving up behind him was that bastard North. Edik stepped right quickly.

"My name," said Lukyanova, her voice still slow and thick as this strange creature's movements, "is Anna Lukyanova, daughter of Alexei Lukyanov. What should I call you?"

The thing stopped moving where it was. If it attempted to speak, Edik heard nothing.

Edik relaxed his vision, opening himself to thaumaturgic impressions. He could feel Dola, of course, then the magic of Jones and North — oddly gratifying that Jones felt stronger than North — nothing in particular from Edmund or Lukyanova, apart from her bracelet, but the thing was a different matter.

This thing was no trick of kinetic spells. A spirit drove it. So it had to have been someone's servitor. The girl's ... no, her self-introduction wouldn't have been necessary. Jones didn't bring it, and Edik doubted that North could have.

"Looks like someone lost their servitor," said Edik. "I'm sure that if we take it back to Kennedy."

"No," said Jones. "That was my first thought too, but look closer."

Lukyanova gave an irritated growl, and Edmund muttered something that must have been commiseration. Or maybe he was putting the moves on Jones' girl, though this would have been an odd time for the effort.

But Edik stretched out a little more with his senses.

And he saw what Jones must have seen. A tight aura, uniformly close to the rocky flesh.

"That glow. It mirrors the Barrier and not just in color."

"It's ... preserving," said North, awe in his gruff voice.

"It's life," said Jones, then louder, to the thing, he said, "You're not just a bound spirit, are you? You're alive, and that's your body, isn't it?"

"Ludicrous," muttered North, a bigger word than Edik expected him to know. Probably just thought it sounded impressive.

But Jones had a point. Bound spirits looked ... contained ... within their bindings. But whatever this thing was, it looked ... at home within its rocky shape. As though this were somehow ... natural for it.

Edik found himself looking at Dola, the closest creature he had ever seen to that strange, rocky tripod thing before them now.

The thing stopped and stared and ... *probed*. It was probing at them. Magically. Animals couldn't do that, though bound spirits could.

"Let go of me," said Lukyanova, shoving Edmund aside and stepping closer to the thing. She moved as though every part of her ached, but she had a steady hand out and spoke in a fairly soothing tone, considering that her words still came out heavy.

"Shhh. It's all right. Nobody's going to hurt you."

"Anna," said Jones, "this might not be a good idea."

But she kept approaching. And maybe it was just the outfit, but she seemed as though she were treating it like a spooked horse, trying to soothe with her tone.

"Don't you worry about them. Nobody means you any harm. We just want to talk to you."

One step at a time she moved closer. The thing arched its — neck? — and twisted its rounded end as it looked at her. Probed at her.

Jones followed her two steps behind and a spell not quite crackling between his fingers.

Then his boot crunched on a piece of shattered red ceramics from the crashed ship.

"No, Carl," she said, still in that same soothing tone and without looking back to see who followed her, "let me do this on my own. If we spook this poor thing, it may bolt."

"And it may strike," Jones said, matching her tone. "We don't know what it can do."

North stepped up beside Edik and muttered in his ear.

"Bet the spell geeks at Kennedy Thaum. would love to get their hands on it. Pay a pretty penny, I bet."

Edik opened his mouth to tell North exactly what he could do with his mercenary ideas.

But the words never made it past his lips.

North might be the most backstabbing, fare-stealing, untrustworthy bastard ever to sail the skies, but Edik, well...

Edik *did* need money.

22

ANNA FELT AS THOUGH HER BRAIN WERE TUCKED WAY DEEP DOWN INSIDE her body, and a layer of that safety foam lay between her brain and her body. It was a good thing she didn't need to move quickly. Every step took forever, and had to end with careful placement of her riding boot, because she couldn't quite feel her feet yet.

Or her legs. Or her arms. Or much of anything else.

She *could* hear her heart beat pounding in her chest, but even that sounded as though layers of cotton lay between her ears and the sound. And it felt even further away than that.

And for the life of her, she thought she must be chilly, out here on a spring evening at the Failed Site outside of Kennedy — nowhere near her intended landing bay — in just her riding clothes. But she didn't feel warm or cold, just ... dulled.

The glow of the Barrier was close enough to give her just enough yellowed light to see by. And she thought she could smell an alkaline mixture including bay leaves and ginger — which was a combination that no one would use these days. But the scent was distant, and the light dimmer than she would have thought.

It was all she could do to keep her words from slurring as she kept up her soft patter at the most fascinating thing she could ever have imagined meeting.

It was alive. It moved. But its body wasn't made of flesh like an animal's. Anna had heard of servitor creatures, spirits bound into formerly inanimate objects like statues, but those were rare. She was pretty sure the Romanovs had one, but Father had said that he would not take a job from one of the servants he employed and give it to some creature born of magic.

Of course, she suspected that Father would not have trusted the magician's motivations in creating such a servitor. Perhaps if her eldest brother, Dmitri — a Journeyman magician himself — were to have created it...

But the three-legged creature before her didn't seem as though it had been created with a purpose at all. And didn't all those servitors have purposes?

Another step. More nonsense soothing words.

The creature tilted its head at her. As though quizzical. As though trying to figure her out as much as she was trying to figure it out. She could hear muffled movement behind her. Carl would keep the others back. She hoped.

He had to trust her that far, didn't he? Even though she had been wrong about Father and Matei? He had to know she could not have predicted their response.

But she could not worry about them. They would do what they would do. Anna could only keep her feet moving, crunching debris and shifting loose gravel with every step. Finding her weight with every step, keeping her slow for as good a reason as keeping the creature calm.

"You can hear, me, can't you?" she said. "Can you understand what I'm saying? Can you understand, at least, that I mean you no harm?"

"Ask it for a sign." Carl's voice. Several steps behind her. That was good.

"If you can understand me, show me. Do this." She stopped moving, then took her forward foot, her left, raised it up and stomped it down. She had to shake to keep her balance, but she didn't quite tip over.

The head tilted back so the two yellow eyes were up top again, as though straightening itself out.

It raised its forward foot and slammed it down. Hard. The cockpit of the airship groaned and cracked. Big rocks shifted. The ground vibrated.

Anna fell.

She heard swords behind her and tried to yell, "No! I'm all right!" but she could only hear blood rushing through the veins near her ears. She had no idea if the words made it out.

But where she sat on the ground, she reached out with one hand toward the creature, palm down and soothing.

"It's all right," she told her tongue to say, though she couldn't quite make out the words that came out. It was as though she had her palms pressed against her ears and someone else was talking.

"It's all right," she tried to say again. "I'm all right. I got a little hurt, when my airship crashed, but I'm all right."

She moved her head down and up, an exaggerated nod.

"If you can understand me, nod like this." She did it again.

A moment later, the creature nodded, swinging its rounded nose up and down.

"It understand me," she called back, and this time she could hear her words.

"No shit," said the gruff, barrel-chested man in uniform. North, if she had understood Carl correctly. The taller man — Barshai, she believed — the one with the roguish good looks and the blonde hair and the clothes like a shadow play pirate, smacked the other on the chest with the back of his hand.

Edmund stood to one side, looking so nervous he might shake apart.

But Carl was smiling. A small, simple smile, as though he shared her delight at what she was pretty sure they had discovered here today — the first sapient, incarnate life form other than the human race.

She met his eye, and for a fleeting moment wished she *had* taken him as a lover. How much greater would their sharing of this moment be?

But that would have been a disaster for them both, if it had worked out at all.

She turned back to the creature. Had it moved a step or two closer?

"Can you speak? Do you have a language?"

"Of course it can speak," said a meter-tall gray cat, so suddenly beside her that she had to brace with an arm to not fall again. And she couldn't be sure in the dim light, but it might have been semi-transparent. "And of course it has a language."

Oh. Of course. Dola. Familiar to either North or Barshai.

"Can you communicate with it?"

The cat opened its mouth to speak, hesitated, then closed its jaws and flattened its ears. It looked back at the others. "Edik?"

"Go ahead," called back one of the captains. If they were both captains. Anna was uncertain on that point.

The cat then turned and said something to the creature, but for the life of her Anna could not understand what. It didn't sound like any language she had ever heard. Not the rolling beauty of Russian, not the practical impracticality of English, not the odd cadences of Congolese, nor the harsh syllables of Gaelic.

It sounded … it sounded like shorthand. As though every vowel and consonant meshed together to abbreviate something longer and more complex. Perhaps as though only half of the communication, or maybe less, took place on the verbal level.

But the break gave her a chance to sit and pull herself together. Her whole body still ached, but she couldn't see any signs of bruising. And she didn't smell blood, which was good, though the bay leaf and ginger smell was stronger than … she … expected…

Anna flared her trained nostrils several times in quick succession. She'd been to the Failed Site twice before, once as part of learning about her new home when they first moved to the moon, and once as an object lesson to those who act without sufficient planning.

She knew well the alkaline smells, with their combination of ginger and bay leaf. Usually the bay leaf was stronger. But right now the ginger smell was much stronger. And underneath that, verbena and hazel. Why did those smells stick out in her mind?

Anna looked over at the creature, its head moving as though deep in conversation with Dola.

Anna sniffed the air again.

No doubt now. Those smells came from the creature.

23

Carl didn't like the whispering going on between Barshai and North while Barshai's familiar "chatted" with the strange creature.

For two men that seemed to be sworn enemies only a few minutes ago, they seemed to be awfully comfortable conspiring together. Leaning toward each other, trying to talk without moving their lips.

And perhaps Carl had spent too many years in the service, but when he saw to apparent enemies huddled together and whispering, he assumed conspiracy. It was just safer.

But Edmund looked to be in earshot, and Carl knew his brother Duane would have made sure to listen in on whatever those two were discussing. So maybe Edmund was playing the safe route and listening in too, though his eyes moved back and forth between Anna and the creature.

At least the familiar seemed to be reasonable enough. Perhaps Carl could persuade it to tell the truth about whatever its conversation with the creature involved. Presuming its master didn't interfere...

Carl grimaced and stepped up to the whispering air pilots.

"Just what is so utterly fascinating that it can't wait?"

"Look," said North, "you can stop us from killing each other right now, but that doesn't mean you get to butt in anytime you want. Go watch your girlfriend. This is none of your business."

Carl looked at Barshai, but Barshai looked away.

Ashamed?

"Let's get something clear right this second," said Carl in clipped, military tones. "That thing back there" — he gestured over his shoulder with his thumb — "that's a person. Not a treasure chest or a prize pig. Clear?"

"Aye fucking aye, *sir*," snapped North with a mocking salute. He turned to Barshai. "First man to call it a prize pig gets ten lashes. Second—"

Carl punched North in the gut, hard enough to bend him forward and knock most of the air out of that barrel chest. A warning shot, really. Otherwise it would have been followed by a lot more pain.

To his left, Barshai laughed.

"Now let's you and me get something straight," said Carl while North gasped for air. "I'm not your friend, I am not your business associate, and I have taken exactly all the shit I'm going to take from you tonight. You insult me one more time, or you try anything with that creature that it or I don't like, and you won't live to duel your old friend Barshai here."

Barshai was still laughing when Carl rounded on him.

"And you," Carl said in cold tones. "I don't know what you're thinking, trying to cut some kind of deal with North here maybe, but I have my eye on you too. So don't do anything stupid."

"What the hell do you care?" said Barshai. "What difference does it make to you if we form a treaty with its people or sell it to the zoo?"

That question pulled Carl up short. He didn't have any reason to care. No one was paying him. He wasn't working for Earth. He wasn't certified for first contact, and he had no contractual, legal, moral, or ethical obligation that he could think of for getting involved with any of this. In fact, given the trouble that Anna had cost him, he had a pretty good reason to turn away and leave this whole mess of trouble to her. Or the captains. Or whoever wanted it.

Because this *was* a whole mess of trouble, and trouble was something Carl already had plenty of. He didn't need to go looking for more.

Except...

Except that this thing wasn't just some bound spirit, or yet another of the countless troubled people on this or any other world that Carl couldn't save. This was right here in front of him, and it was something he'd never seen before, never heard of before.

At its core, whatever that creature was, it was just what he had called it while shaming Barshai, who still looked flush around the neck at Carl's words. This three-legged, apparently mouthless mass of moving rock wasn't just some "it," some creature to be dissected by the curious or displayed to the thrill-seeking.

This was a person. It had language. Communication. It might even have family, maybe a brother off somewhere that was as much like Duane as a tripedal rock creature could be.

Maybe it was alone and scared, or lost, or maybe even the only one of its kind.

But whatever it was, it needed help and had no one else to turn to.

It needed a champion, and, well, that was what the title on Carl's identification read — licensed champion.

But in answer to Barshai's question, he said, "Maybe I care, or maybe I don't. But I tell you right now that this creature is a foreigner here and doesn't know our ways or our laws. It needs an interpreter, and as far as I can tell that's your familiar."

"Probably any familiar could do the same thing, but yeah, I'm fine with Dola taking on that role."

"And me," said Carl, "I'm going to make sure it gets fair treatment, whatever that may be."

"Suppose," said North, words strained and one hand on his belly as he straightened up, "that Barshai and me disagree that you deserve any role in this at all."

"Oh, enough grandstanding," called back Anna, who was on her feet now and walking back toward the rest of the group, Dola by her side. "Stop hitting and threatening each other for five minutes."

Dola chuckled and said something to Barshai in that odd speech that familiars shared with their magicians.

"It wants us to call it Oolaut," continued Anna, "and it's lost. It's not sure how it got here, and it wants to go back to the others."

"There are others?" said Barshai, meeting glances with North.

"Many," said Dola.

"So it doesn't need much from us," said Anna, disappointment in her voice, but moving and sounding better than she had yet. The sluggish effects of the safety foam had to have been wearing off, though she still stepped and moved gingerly. Probably full of aches. "It just needs a lift."

"The others," said Dola in plain English, "are somewhere close to the Pillar, if you can believe that."

"I'll handle it then," said North. "Know just where the Pillar is. Maybe even a good guess at where these things gather. So I'll just take it from here and the rest of you—"

"You don't honestly think that's going to work," said Carl, "do you?"

"He might be that stupid," said Barshai, tugging at his blonde Van Dyke.

"Hey!" said North. "I'm just trying to help us all out here. No need for Barshai and me both to burn fuel for this."

"I agree," said Barshai, "and since Dola and Anna are the only ones who've spoken to it — and since her airship is in no condition to fly — it only makes sense that Oolaut fly home aboard the *Third Son*. So I guess, you, North, might as well go home."

"Not a chance." North shook his head hard enough that his shaggy hair and beard whipped around. "You're not leaving me out."

"We've got this," said Barshai. "Run along home."

North's hand went to his cutlass.

Honestly, how did this man make it through a week without someone killing him?

"Stop," said Carl with a sigh. "Both of you. Anna's right. We've had enough grandstanding for one day, even from me. North, you were here when we all met Oolaut, so cutting you out of taking him" — Carl looked at Dola and Anna — "is Oolaut a him?"

"We're not sure on pronouns," said Anna, while Dola nodded.

Carl turned back to North without missing a beat. "So we're not cutting you out of escorting Oolaut home. You can ride in the *Third Son* with the rest of us."

"No he can not," said Barshai.

"Then he flies the rest of us there about the *Sparrow*." Carl shrugged. "Up to you, really."

North couldn't have given Barshai a more needling, satisfied grin if the sick bastard had slept with Barshai's wife, sister and mother all in the same night.

"You stick to the common areas," said Barshai, shoving a finger in North's broad chest. "I'm not letting you on the bridge, and you better not go anywhere near the engine or I'll spike your body on the tip of the Pillar."

24

EDIK SETTLED INTO HIS PILOT SEAT ABOARD THE *THIRD SON*, CALLED UP the phantasmal workspace, and ran through the latest reports of the skies around Kennedy. He'd taken a moment to bandage the cut on his hand, but now he had to get on with the business of flying.

Nothing but usual traffic, which meant only flights going into and out of the port right now. No one flying tours to the surrounding area after dark, so the odds were pretty good of Edik setting his ship down somewhere close to the Pillar without drawing any curious onlookers. And as the oddest rock configuration on Luna, the Pillar almost always drew a crowd.

The lingering smell of old borscht, usually a comfort on long flights, only served to make his stomach growl and remind him that he could use some dinner. That moonfish and chips was hours ago.

Rain coming in, but from the north, so it shouldn't bother them, provided they finished this little jaunt before midnight. They were west of Kennedy proper right now, and Edik could take a southern route around to the east and the Pillar. Light airs, but nothing much more than that. Few drops maybe.

One odd news alert. Missing ... child...

Edik spun in his chair and looked over at Dola, sitting just inside the gold-colored cabin door. "Missing child report."

"You don't have to open it," said Dola. A ripple passed down his gray fur. "You aren't accountable for information you don't have."

"I can see the name Lukyanov in the teaser, and a mention of the word 'kidnapping.' You don't think they could call us to account for that? Her being aboard this ship — this *helioship* — and all."

"Far as we know," said Dola, whiskers twitching the way they did when he thought he was getting away with something, "she's past the age of majority. Means she's not a child. She could buy her own drinks, rent her own ships. Could be she's got a kid brother who vanished today. The point is—"

"The point is you like her."

"I didn't say that." Dola's ears gave a guilty twitch.

"One, she may already be dating Carl. Two—"

"By the bound heart of Koschei the Deathless, I don't want you to *date* her. She's a good ten years younger than you are."

"Then what—"

"It's just nice to get some female perspective around here." Dola crossed his paws and hunkered down. "You need to date someone, Edik. You spend too much time with just me and your elementals. You need companionship among your own people."

"Hardly the time to discuss my sex life."

"You need one of those too."

Edik narrowed his eyes. Dola didn't blink, his own eyes the picture of cerulean serenity. Edik growled. Still no response.

Finally Dola broke into a hissing snicker, and Edik sighed and slumped forward, elbows on his knees.

"Did you just come up with that or did you set up the whole conversa—"

"I've been waiting to use that one on you for days."

"It came out rehearsed."

"*It did not.*" Dola's tail twitched. "Anyway, you *do* need to start dating. And I *do* like her. She's smart, and just listening to her talk I can tell she's better at alchemy that you are." Dola tilted his head. "But then, who isn't?"

Edik spun back around in his chair to see about getting his ship off the ground. The sooner this business was done, the sooner he'd be rid of the overzealous licensed champion, the possible missing child, and that fare-stealing bastard. Speaking of which...

"Maybe you better get back there and keep an eye on North."

"Nixia's got it. Besides, North would keep an eye on me right back."

Edik shook his head and tapped the rear section of the miniature firebird display, alerting the air elementals of the planetary engine to prepare for flight. The hour was growing late faster than Edik would have preferred anyway. Especially since that duel was interrupted and he couldn't count on getting any money out of North for three more days.

Getting that odd stone creature — Oolaut, if Dola got the name right...

...all right. That wasn't fair. Edik had no reason to take out his frustration with North on his familiar, even if it did make fun of him too much. No doubt Dola had gotten the name right, or provided a pronunciation as close as human tongues could manage.

Anyway, getting the creature onto the *Third Son* had already wasted a solid half hour — a portion of that just for Dola to tell it what was involved and almost all of the rest for Anna Lukyanova to reassure herself or it that this was a good idea and Oolaut would be safe.

But finally it entered the main cabin, and even now perched on one of Edik's padded passenger chairs. Which looked awkward, but would keep Oolaut protected by the basic, Luna-mandated kinetic dampening spell that would keep it from spilling out onto the floor during the flight.

The others better be wearing their five-point safety belts. Especially North. If he tried to claim any injury...

No. North wasn't that stupid. But then, he *was* stupid enough to try a trick like using the head and then pulling some little spell to slip past Nixia and into restricted areas below decks.

Jones seemed to have his number though, and Jones didn't seem to care for North any more than Edik did.

No. Edik could probably count on Jones to keep North from wandering into any off-limits areas. Even if he found a way past Nixia.

"Throws a pretty good punch," said Edik as he eased the *Third Son* into the air with a mighty flap of its wings. "Wouldn't you say?"

"I'm glad he didn't hit *you*. I might have had to intervene, and I wouldn't want to see what he could do with a spell."

"Barely feels like an Initiate to me." Scanners read clear sky, and Edik couldn't see anything but the Kennedy Barrier from here. The stars were where they ought to be, which Edik always took comfort in. Safe to head out as soon as he—

"That's what I mean. He *feels* like an Initiate who barely passed his exams. But I don't believe it. There's something about him that twitches my whiskers."

Edik glanced back over his shoulder, his hand hesitating on the airborne accelerator.

"What are you saying?"

"I'm not sure." Dola's fur ruffled. "It's like he can hide how good he is. But I'm not sure. I've never seen anything like that before."

Edik tried to puzzle through how that could be — private tutoring and some native talent for deception magic perhaps — but the comm pad flashed red, indicating a call from a local ship. Sure enough, another ship was coming straight at him, though still outside the Barrier. It looked like a dark, faux-metal cylinder with all the edges rounded and a stack of three big boxes, top and center.

Edik had seen an image like that in a museum back in San Francisco. From before the rise of magic. A sub-marine?

It looked a little big to just be an airship.

Edik felt an uncomfortable tingle on the back of his neck.

He tapped the comm pad, opening the communication link.

"Attention, *Third Son*, this is the *Kiev*." Official sounding voice. A woman. "You are departing the scene of an accident involving the *Morning's Glory*, please—"

Another voice took over. A man's angry baritone.

"*Third Son* this is Alexei Lukyanov, and that crashed ship is mine. Just where the hell do you think you're going with my daughter?"

25

TRAPPED.

How could Father have found her so quickly?

Anna's hands pulled at the five-point safety belts locking her to a chair that had felt deep and comfortable only moments ago.

Now it felt like quicksand, pulling her down. Her heart pounded and the air in the *Third Son's* main cabin felt unaccountably warm, as though the huge, glowing red feather on the ceiling generated heat as well as light.

But Anna's school training minimized her outside signs of stress. A trickle of sweat between her shoulder blades, but not a drop on her forehead. Breathing still slow and deep, despite the jangling of her nerves, because there were eyes on her in a public place.

A Lukyanova could feel fear. Fear had its uses. But none must ever see that fear. An early lesson from childhood grown into reflex over time and training. She could not even blush in a public place, not even under the leer of that awful Captain North.

Edmund didn't leer, but his eyes kept coming to rest on her. They glanced everywhere, not just at the other passengers, as though the ship itself fascinated him as much as even Oolaut did. But still, as he sat in his passenger seat with effortless elegance, his eyes kept coming to rest on her.

Interested. She could tell. And he had the good looks and poise to go with what seemed to be a gentle nature. Anna rarely got to meet men like him, not at the kind of social events Father required of her. Under other circumstances, Anna would have smiled. Flirted.

But Father was here. This was no time for games.

Carl's eyes were on her too. Not leering or flirting, of course, but not judging either. Not even gloating, which he had a right to do. He simply observed her, as he had no doubt observed the slight pomegranate scent to the air, a suggestion that Captain Barshai used gentle bindings for his air and earth elementals.

Maybe Carl studied her reaction, or her lack of any obvious reaction. Either way, he had watched her ever since Dola poked his head through the cockpit door and announced that they were landing again in response to a formal request from Alexei Lukyanov.

Why couldn't Captain Barshai have been the space pirate he looked like? Then he could have flown off. Led Father on a merry chase, then a narrow escape and she could have been free once and for all.

Two days in Kennedy and no one she knew would have recognized her.

But no, Anna could not blame Captain Barshai for landing. He had to live and work here on Luna. He could not disappear as easily as she could. And Father could have run him out of business, perhaps even off of Luna entirely, with so little effort he might not have noticed he'd done it, except to take pleasure in crushing someone who defied him.

Anna had defied him. Publicly. No doubt Father looked forward to crushing her too.

Anna looked over at Oolaut. Those disc-like yellow eyes stared back at her, and she could not begin to guess what went on behind them. Did it have anything like human thoughts or feelings? Did it know how she worried about it? Understand that she, perhaps more than the others, *wanted* to make sure it got home safely.

Those eyes looked away then, the narrowed, rounded — head? Snout? — twisted and turned, looking along edges and seems of the ship, but what it saw she couldn't guess.

Anna set her jaw, drew her posture even straighter than habit kept it. Yes, she had run away from home. Yes, she had stolen and crashed Father's airship. But if she had not done those things, poor Oolaut might still be wandering lost.

Father might be able to make her come back home. Father might be able to do a great many things. But Father could not stop her from seeing this strange, incarnate spirit back to others like itself. She would walk it home alone if she had to.

And if Father tried to stop her, then Father could find out just how strong a will he had instilled in his youngest daughter.

Anna felt the *Third Son* land and settle onto the rough, strange ground of the Failed Site in likely just about the same location it had occupied previously. Almost jarring. She hadn't realized she'd been able to feel the descent, a mere slight lift in her stomach, until it wasn't there anymore.

North was out of his seat faster than Anna could release the first point on her safety belt. Carl was only a moment behind him. The cockpit door slid open and Dola trotted in, warning Captain North again about behaving himself. As though this warning would somehow have more effect than the others.

Anna was finally free and on her feet when Captain Barshai entered the main cabin. Edmund, she noted with some pleasure, couldn't get free of his restraints any faster than she had.

"All right," Captain Barshai said, and pointed to the ... hull. Hadn't there been a hatch door there earlier? Smooth work. "Before we go meet whatever storm is coming for us, let's figure out where we stand."

"What's to discuss?" said Captain North, with a shrug of those huge shoulders. "The guy wants his daughter, I'm not going to stand in his way. But then," — he leered at Carl — "*I'm* not the one fucking her."

Carl's eyes barely narrowed, and Anna would have sworn his jaw didn't move, but his expression darkened in a way that she would have sworn promised pain to the rude airship captain.

Captain North grinned, and Anna had to resist the urge to shiver with disgust.

"Well, Jones?" said Captain Barshai. "Do you intend to stand in his way?"

Carl didn't answer. He just looked at Anna, his eyes relaxing into that patient look he had. The same one he gave her after explaining that her plan to get out of marriage to Ivan Romanov wouldn't work, but she insisted on going ahead with it.

"I won't ask any of you to fight for me." A pang of guilt made her look at Carl. "Any more than you have already." She shook her head. "But I'm not going back with him."

"Tall order," said Captain Barshai. "Do you have any idea just how much clout your father really has?"

"I assure you," she said, "I have an even better sense of it than you believe you do. But that doesn't matter." She pointed at Oolaut, who watched her while Dola translated the whole conversation in hushed tones. "I will see Oolaut home, and Father will not stop me."

"Big words," said Captain North. "I—"

"I'm sure we all know what you think," said Carl. "If you can call what you do *thinking*."

"Shut up, North," said Captain Barshai. "We don't have time for Jones here to cut you to ribbons, however much I might enjoy the process, even at the cost of the money I intend to recover from you."

"Good luck with that," said Captain North.

"Jones," said Captain Barshai, pointed turning away from Captain North. "Where do you stand?"

"Oolaut needs all the help he can get. What more is there to say?"

"Doesn't mean Oolaut needs her. We can fly it—"

"I *will* help," insisted Anna.

"Enough!" said Edmund. "Please. Let's go talk to Anna's father. He's probably just worried about the crash. Maybe he'll be reasonable when he finds out that his daughter's fine, and he may even help with Oolaut."

"You don't know my father," said Anna.

Someone thumped on the hatch.

Dola said something. Anna couldn't understand it, but Captain Barshai nodded.

"All right," said Captain Barshai. "North, you want in on this Oolaut business, then you have to stand with us now. Otherwise you're out."

Carl nodded, and Edmund followed his lead. Captains North and Barshai locked glares, but finally Captain North gave a grudging nod.

"All right," said Captain Barshai as someone thumped on the hatch again. "I'd say we're ready."

26

CARL HAD BARELY SET HIS BLACK LOAFERS BACK ON THE SICKLY GREEN rock of the Failed Site when he decided this was the worst set up for a skirmish he'd ever been on the wrong side of.

Starry night sky with not much more than the dark yellow glow of the Barrier keeping the lighting dim and visibility short. Little breeze coming in from the north, but not enough wind to get in anyone's eyes.

On his side, Barshai, with more will than technique, though maybe he'd do better in a brawl than a formal duel; North, who had the muscles and the scars to be an asset if he felt like it, but who lacked motivation. He'd likely throw down his sword at the first real opportunity and howl about how he'd been forced to fight.

That was it for their assets. Edmund held his chin high and his chest out, but the look in his eyes said he'd rather be hiding or running. Might do either if a fight broke out. Anna would get in the middle of things and probably get herself hurt or worse, which meant that Carl would have to keep an eye on her, putting himself at greater risk.

Dola was likely to be useless in a fight. Most familiars were.

Oolaut ... unpredictable. Carl just hoped he or she or whatever it was just stayed on the ship and out of sight. The last thing Carl wanted was for the head of one of Luna's powerful families to get their hands on Oolaut and its people.

And on the other side was the real trouble, starting with Alexei Lukyanov himself. Not much taller than his daughter, but solid, with a Dalca saber at his side and a reputation that said he knew how to use it. He was dressed for a funeral, black suit and tie, even his shirt was a deep, somber blue. Next to him stood a magician with enough power flowing around him to be a Magister. Taller, with short hair as blonde as Anna's and the chin, nose and eyes that proclaimed him Alexei Lukyanov's son as loudly as any birth certificate could. Dressing like his father only aided the resemblance.

Two formidable men on their own. But they weren't alone. They had six men with them, all in black shirts, slacks and ankle boots like Matei Negrescu had been, though without the tie. Three fanned out to Lukyanov's right, and three more to his son's left. And those men held black billy clubs. Pacifiers, and they didn't feel like civilian-grade. Odds were that even a close swipe with one of those could suck the fight right out of an opponent.

Behind them was that submarine-like ship, some sixty meters long and twenty high. Had to be a helioship. Nobody made pure airships that big or that un-aerodynamic.

The ship didn't matter right now. Not on the ground. The men did.

There was a trick magicians could use to counter Pacifiers. Carl knew how to do it, but six was a large number, and he couldn't count on Barshai or North even knowing the trick, much less having the skill to implement it. Not with their educations restricted mainly to handling the magic of their ships.

Not for the first time Carl wished he'd taken the time to find a private tutor who could further his own training. And if he were taking the time to wish, he'd wish that he'd had something more than a few apples slices to eat since Zira's. Even a turkey sandwich would have been welcome.

But this was not the time for wishes.

Lukyanov barked something at his daughter. Sounded Russian. She answered in English.

"No, Father. The Romanovs canceled the wedding, and you want to ruin what's left of my life."

North grumbled something about spoiled children.

"You're ruining it right now, Anya," said her brother, in gentle tones.

"No, Dimi." Fire in her voice to match her words. "I am making my own choices as you did."

Anna's brother — Dimi — went as still as Anna had been when word came that her father was here. She must have struck a nerve.

"You are being foolish, as always," said Lukyanov, "and I am in no mood for games. You have shamed your family, made a mockery of Matya's funeral, and now I find you flying off with your lover and this … this disreputable group? No. I will not stand for it. Come along *right now*."

Lukyanov started to turn away, and his son turned with him. But Anna said, simply, "No."

Lukyanov and his son stopped mid-step, then each set his dress shoe down slowly.

They turned back, just as slowly.

"No?" said Lukyanov. "Is that what I heard you say to me?" He rattled off something in Russian that Carl couldn't guess at, but from the way Anna's brother looked away, it must have been scathing.

"No," she said again, holding herself with perfect poise. Only a moistening to her eyes gave any sign that Lukyanov's words had gotten to her. "And your insults are beneath you, Father."

"Dimitri," said Lukyanov, but before he could finish the sentence, Carl cut in.

"Stop right there. Anna, you're eighteen, am I right?"

"Yes," she said, puzzled.

"That makes her an adult and a citizen of Luna. That means she has the freedom to go where she chooses, when she chooses, and no one, not even her father, has any legal right to compel her."

"What is it with this guy and the law?" North whispered too loudly to Barshai.

"Ah, the lover speaks," said Lukyanov, finally turning to look at Carl. "So you are the man my Anya has cast her family aside for."

"I haven't cast—"

"A trained killer. Military and special services, I understand. Tell me, killer, does my daughter know how many lives you've taken?"

"I only wanted—" Emotion was starting to crackle through her anger, but Lukyanov's attention was on Carl now.

"Or is that not the pillow talk you choose when seducing little girls into your bed. Because a virgin at eighteen may be an adult by law, but you and I both know she is still a child."

Those tears were flowing down Anna's face now, but Carl held his temper in check. Wasn't easy with adrenaline starting to pulse through his system. With old habits telling him the order of his targets and the techniques he should use. His fingers itched for a handle in his hand.

Especially with the words of Natalia Romanova in his head, reminding him how much she would pay him for the death of Alexei Lukyanov. Yes, she had wanted the death to come in a duel, but if Lukyanov started a fight, that might come close enough...

But Carl clenched his jaw and held his silence.

"Nothing?" said Lukyanov, bushy eyebrows comically high. "Not a word to defend yourself? Or are you simply man enough to accept the truth when you hear it?"

"Father, stop," said Anna, but it wasn't more than a whisper.

"Or perhaps you are no man at all. Dmitri—"

"He starts to cast, he dies," said Carl, and the words came out sharper than he meant them to.

For a moment, all was silence. Even the breeze stopped.

"I mean it," said Carl, words even now, tone back under control while adrenaline made him jittery. "I'm not going to chance him putting the bunch of us to sleep and you slitting my unconscious throat. I'm not going to find out the hard way that he's got some magical hook in Anna to compel her to leave with you."

Carl drew the slender, well-balanced knife from his boot, with his left hand, leaving his right free for his sword. Not to mention three other knives in easy reach. He held the knife in a throwing grip.

"Not one of you is fast enough to keep me from sinking this in his windpipe, or his jugular, or anywhere else I want to put it." Carl's preferred target was the eye, which was exactly why he didn't mention it. "You've done your homework about me, Lukyanov. You want to risk that I'm bluffing?"

"You would steal my daughter and kill my eldest son on the same day?"

"I won't let you take her against her will and I won't let you kill me."

"Whoa, whoa, whoa," said Edmund, stepping into Carl's line of fire, hands raised. "Let's just ... stop all the killing talk, all right? Nobody's killing anybody. Nobody's taking anybody against their will. All right?"

Carl sighed and relaxed his grip. Lukyanov gazed at Edmund as though one of his servants had dared to offer his opinion about a potential investment opportunity.

"Look," said Edmund, trying to seize his momentary advantage. "Anna's not running away with anybody, okay? Her ship crashed here, and then we all found—"

"No!" said Carl.

"That's enough!" said Barshai.

"Shut up!" said North.

"Edmund, no!" said Anna.

The sudden outpouring of dissent brought Edmund to a stumbling silence.

But then Lukyanov said, with entirely too much interest for Carl's taste, "Found what?"

27

"LOOK," SAID EDIK, STEPPING FORWARD AND RAISING HIS OWN HANDS TO match Edmund. He had to hand it to Edmund. The boy had courage. Out here in the Failed Site, at night yet, where a family like the Lukyanovs could have killed pretty much anybody and gotten away with it, and the kid was still willing to step forward and try to de-escalate matters.

Of course, it had been Jones, not Lukyanov, who mentioned killing. Lukyanov just left the threat of it implicit in the air. Breeding, Edik supposed.

"Look," Edik said again as the wind picked back up, chillier and a little stronger now, carrying not just the bay leaves and alkaline smell for the Failed Site, but the first hints of rain that shouldn't arrive for a couple of hours yet. "All she found was help." Edik tilted his head, as though he'd have to admit getting caught at something. "All right, she also happened to find North and me making a business deal, but it's just a tourism thing. Nothing you'd be—"

"You're a reasonably good liar," said Lukyanov, "but not nearly good enough for this. Just what did my daughter, the youngest member of the Lukyanov family and the apple of my eye no matter what she thinks of herself, just what did she *find*?"

"Well," said Edmund, but Edik spoke over him.

"She didn't find anything. We all found it. And it's nothing you'd be interested in, believe me."

"I am interested in a great many things," said Lukyanov, stepping forward, eyeing the *Third Son* in a way that Edik didn't like at all. "Something on your ship, I think, *da*?"

He continued in Russian then, but his words were too fast and his accent too thick for Edik to follow. Too many years had passed since he had spoken the language with any frequency or depth.

But Anna seemed to understand him perfectly. And Anna shook her head slowly, jaw set in that defiant way of hers.

"Clear enough for me," said Jones. Edik didn't like the look of Jones right now. He looked ready to fight, and then some.

No, that wasn't quite it. Edik felt ready to fight. His blood was pumping, his muscles twitching. But Jones looked ready to kill. It was like some darkness had swallowed up the chocolate brown of the man's irises.

For the first time, Edik honestly felt afraid of Jones.

"We have numbers," said Lukyanov, addressing Jones. "Even you cannot throw a dagger with six Pacifiers coming for you."

North drew his cutlass.

"*Whoa!*" said Edmund, hands coming up again. "Everybody take a step back and calm down."

"I could arrange that," said Dmitri, his eyes on Jones.

"No," said Edmund. "No spells. No daggers. No Pacifiers. No swords. For Christ's sake, we're all adults here. Maybe we could try acting like it."

"Now this one has heart," said Lukyanov to Anna. "No family, of course, so I could never have let you marry him, but at least you would not have thrown away your body on a—"

"No more taunts or insults either." But Edmund's voice was shakier now, and his skin was flushed. "Let's all just take a step back, calm down, and try to talk like civilized people."

Jones did the last thing Edik expected. He shrugged and took a step back. Edik did the same. North grumbled, but sheathed his cutlass and took a big step back. Anna's step back was small, but her eyes were locked with her father's when she did it.

Her brother was the first on the other side to take a step back, but the moment he did it the six house guards did it too.

Finally, Lukyanov took a step back.

"Better, see?" said Edmund, voice still shaky. "Now, Edik's right. *Anna* didn't find anything. *We all* found something. But it seems that the others don't agree with sharing that information, so it's not my place to tell you. You'll have to hear it from Anna later."

Lukyanov scowled.

"Boy," he said, "you have heart but not much sense. None of you have my resources. You couldn't possibly exploit whatever find you..." Lukyanov frowned, then turned to his son. "You said the *Morning's Glory* crashed near here, yes? So whatever they *found* they found when *my* airship crashed."

Now Lukyanov was smiling, but Edik had no intention of letting him finish his logic chain.

"Moot point," he said. "We didn't find metals or minerals. You know there's nothing to find here at the Failed Site. If there were, the site might not have failed."

"But you found something, where nothing has ever been found before. Also where no ship has ever crashed before. The connection is inescapable."

"And irrelevant," said Anna. "No treasure has been found here, Father. No mine, nothing to claim or profit from."

North grumbled, but Anna pressed on. "Dimi, I have never been able to lie to you. Not about anything small, and not about anything big. If Father doesn't believe me, you tell us all right now. Am I lying?"

"You've told the truth," her brother said without hesitation. "But you haven't told the whole truth either, Anya."

"That's only because we did find something. But nothing we will profit from."

"Pure truth, Father," said Dimitri, softly.

"No," said Lukyanov. "*She* might not intend to profit, but she flies with a mercenary and two pilots, at least one of whom is blatant in his desire to profit from this venture."

"Of course I am," barked North. "I don't have your name, your lands or your fortune. All I've got is my ship and the living I can make from it. Just like Barshai here. Ain't either one of us does a damn thing he doesn't see profit in."

Edik was just about to cut him off, but North got even louder.

"*But*, the profit that puts food on *our* tables for a night isn't enough to feed your prize stallions. Men like us live and die on less money than you lose in a night's gambling."

"I do not gamble," said Lukyanov, "but I take your point."

He looked around at the assemblage. Jones met his eye, and Edik wondered for a moment just how many people Jones had killed. Still, Edik knew what Lukyanov saw: two tour pilots, a licensed champion, a kid still finding his way, and his own daughter.

Lukyanov sighed.

"Anya, you are making a grave mistake. Your killer will break your heart."

"No, Father, he won't."

Edik narrowed his eyes. She didn't sound like a woman in love, and Jones didn't act like a protective lover. Whatever was between them, Edik doubted it involved sex.

"Very well then," Lukyanov continued, shaking his head. "Some lessons you must learn yourself. My door is not closed to you, Anya, but if you come home, you must find a true way to help your family. No more of this alchemy nonsense."

Alchemy? Edik turned and looked at Anna, seeing past the young woman who seemed exactly what North kept calling her — a spoiled brat — and wondering just who Edik had pulled out of that safety foam.

"I would not ask you to give up poker, Father, or your businesses, or your swordplay. Do not ask me to give up alchemy."

Lukyanov set his jaw and gave a heavy sigh through his nose. He shook his head, turned, and walked away toward his ship. Dimitri looked at Anna for a moment, then held up a fist, as if telling her to stay strong. Then he too turned and left.

The guards followed, backing away and keeping themselves between Jones and Dmitri.

"Now can we please get this over with?" asked North. "I've had about all the family drama I can take for one day."

Edik expected to see tears when he looked over at Anna, but she stood still and perfect as a painting, and watched her father's ship lift off and fly away.

28

A~NNA~ ~FOUND~ ~THAT~ ~SHE~ ~RELISHED~ ~THE~ ~SAFETY~ ~BELTS~ ~STRAPPING~ ~HER~ ~TO~ the passenger chair this time. The *Third Son* had lifted off again, and she took comfort in the way the straps held her to the chair. As though she were tiny once more, clasped in tight to the great brown teddy bear Ursa, who was even bigger than she was.

Once upon a time she would press her little body back against her teddy bear, and clasp his arms around her waist. As though Ursa's protective embrace could keep her safe from all harm, or even too much feeling.

And Anna had too much feeling to deal with just then. She felt so much inner turmoil about Father, about Dimi, about the fight that almost happened and, most of all, the fact that Father had not cast her out.

That she could not believe. It was more than she could have dared hope for, even if returning would have meant negotiating a future she could not stand. Father had left *her* the option. The same man who had cast out her middle brother Rodion. Poor Rodya. No one in the family was even permitted to speak his name aloud. He had quarreled with father five years ago, and when he left Father had declared that Rodion would never return.

Anna had felt certain, positive, that Father would declare the same about her. But he had not.

It was all too much. But Anna sat in the eye of the storm. Yes, the emotions were all still there, and yes, the turmoil would catch up with her, but just in that very moment, she felt a pressurized sort of clarity.

And in that state she could look into the eyes of Oolaut and almost, *almost* believe she could see something she understood. A consciousness. A personality. Perhaps even emotion. Something she could recognize.

But if it spoke, she never heard.

Captain North was back to leering at her. Edmund had the look of a boy trying to find the right thing to say, constantly on the verge of speech, but with no words coming out.

Edmund had been brave, standing up to Father and Carl at the same time.

Anna wondered where he found such courage, but she could not ask. Not now. She needed to hold herself in the eye of her emotional storm, not risk bumping up against more emotion that could plunge her into the middle of her own personal tempest. Especially not here, in front of near-strangers. She was a Lukyanova still. Father had not taken that away from her...

Carl had retreated into himself. Literally. He sat with both legs folded under him on the passenger chair, and his eyes closed. Meditating. Anna remembered little about meditation, from the short time that tutors attempted to teach her more than the theory behind thaumaturgy.

All magicians meditated, according to her tutors. Meditation was said to be important to magicians' control and their power.

If it would help Anna hold onto control in situations like this one, she should have paid more attention to that portion of the lessons.

"So tell me, girl," said Captain North, voice quiet and eyes flicking to Carl as though hoping not to draw his attention. "What is it about your boy there? If it's the muscles, I've got muscles. And if you like 'em dangerous—"

"I could not possibly be any less interested in you than I already am," she said, "though I have no doubt that if you keep talking you'll prove me wrong. That there are depths of disinterest I have yet to plumb."

Edmund chuckled, and to her surprise, so did Captain North. Though the latter still made the sound lascivious.

"Come on, girl," he said. "'s obvious that it's over between the two of you. He got what he wanted," — Captain North stroked his gruff beard — "or maybe you got what you wanted. Either way, you're plainly unattached, and interested in older men who have the capacity for violence."

Simple refusal was clearly not enough for this man.

Edmund looked as though he wanted to say something, but bless him he was smart enough to let her handle this herself. Captain North was far from the first undesirable admirer she had had to dissuade since puberty began ensuring that she filled out her clothes as well as her mother did.

Anna finally sighed and turned to look at Captain North. He grinned.

"Did you know," she said, "that for every alchemical bond there is an alchemical solvent?"

Captain North's brow furrowed.

"By which I mean, with all due respect, Captain North, that if you do not stop coming on to me, you will give me no choice but to visit your airship in the middle of the night and dissolve the bonds that hold your ship together." She fluttered her eyelashes and gave him a small smile. "Do we understand each other?"

Captain North gave a loud, raucous guffaw.

"Aw, I do like 'em feisty," he said, clapping his knee with a big hand. "But have it your way, girl, I'll leave you alone for now. Sooner or later, though, you'll be wanting a piece of me, you can bet on it."

He had the gall to wink.

"One more thing," Anna said, letting the sweetness drip out of her tone and something cold replace it. "You will not address me as 'girl.' You will address me as Miss Lukyanova. Do I make myself clear?"

Captain North let out with another guffaw, and this time Oolaut stared at him curiously. The laugh went on and on, to the point that Edmund cleared his throat as an attempt at interruption, but nothing would stop the raucous sound until it had run its course.

Finally the captain spoke again. "Right you are then. *Miss Lukyanova* it is. Right up until you ask me to call you something more ... private."

"North," said Carl without opening his eyes, "do shut up. Your sleaze is intruding on my meditation."

Captain North and Carl exchanged a few harsh words, and while they did, Edmund leaned closer to Anna and asked, quietly, "Could you really just dissolve his ship like that?"

"It's not nearly as easy as I made it sound. Those things have a thousand failsafes. But you'd be surprised how many magicians don't know things like that."

29

"It's never easy," lamented Edik, from the pilot's seat of the *Third Son*. "Why can't it be easy just once in a while? You know, for the shock value?"

"Shocks like that could cause heart attacks," said Dola, voice distracted as he looked over what Edik had just spotted on the scanners.

The *Kiev*. Thousands of meters above them and hundreds behind, but mirroring every pitch and yaw of the *Third Son*.

"Must not have realized this is a helioship," said Dola. "They're probably outside scanner range for most airships."

"I hate being followed when I don't have room to maneuver," said Edik. Right now he kept his ship level at two kilometers up, high enough to avoid the occasional peaks, but low enough not to get noticed ... by Port Authority...

"Get me Kennedy Spaceport Control," he said, while adjusting his course to lead wide of the Pillar, as though he were headed for Petrograd. Right now the ship was due south of Kennedy, and Petrograd would be a more believable destination along this route than any of the smaller places like Jackieville.

Dola reached into the snarl of glowing blue, illusory strands above the comm pad and hooked a single strand with a single claw. He twisted, and a harried young face appeared above the console. A face Edik didn't recognize. Male, with the skin tone and cheekbones to be Korean. The poor kid was in the middle of snapping at someone, but whatever he said wasn't directed along the right angle to carry through the link.

Edik wondered how they managed that, but only with the idle curiosity he often felt about branches of magic he hadn't studied.

Finally, the young man faced Edik. "Kennedy Port Control, this is Cho."

"Hi, Cho, this is Captain Edik Barshai of the *Third Son*, Luna permit number C118J8767F. I've got a helioship on my scanners, the *Kiev*, and it looks like it's following me. Can you check it out?"

"The *Kiev* has an official, logged flight route," the boy said too quickly. His thin eyebrows drew together, forming what Edik thought of as the "liar's line" between them, something that showed up when a person uncomfortable with lying had been obliged to do so. "So I'm sure it's coincidence. I note that you, however, have not logged any current flight route, *Third Son*. Can I get your destination and time of arrival?"

"No," said Edik, glancing back at the scanners and noting that the *Kiev* had indeed shifted course to match. No doubt at all then. "I won't be touching space proper, and I'm flying under the mandatory report ceiling."

"According to Kennedy Spaceport Code Section thirty-three dash one, subsection one bee—"

"You have the authority to ask for a report from any helioship on this side of Luna, I know." Edik itched to accelerate, to dip down closer to the surface and try to lose the trailing ship. But if he did, he'd alert them that he could see them. The fingers of his left hand drummed on the console as he contemplated this, while he finished answering the port communications rookie. "However, as I am flying a private charter, on a route for which no tickets have been sold and public interest not aroused, I am entitled to refuse to answer."

"I don't see—"

"Check the annotations. Look for the Luna's Court's official interpretation of the law. Five years ago the Romanovs, Lukyanovs, and Raskolnikovs sued to keep their movements private from the general populace. The court ruled in their favor, and reaffirmed it last year. Nothing in the ruling says it only applies to the rich."

Edik winked at the poor, harried kid. If the kid had been more savvy, he might have tried a safety angle. Might even have worked with another pilot.

But this Cho was a rookie, and he was hampered from probing at the bidding of the powerful by a sense of honesty and fair play. Edik hoped the kid managed to keep that, if he stuck around. Luna needed more honest civil servants.

"But—"

"Sorry, Port Control, but I have no copilot. I need to cut the line now. Thanks for the update."

Edik swiped a hand through the illusory head of the overmatched kid and cut the link.

"So," said Dola, "not only are the Lukyanovs following us, they're going through official channels to find out where we're going."

"I think old man Lukyanov believes we found something interesting."

"What are you going to do about it?"

"What else?" He shot Dola a grin and pulled back on the illusory pitch control for a gradual ascent. "Go ask him."

"Is this your call, Edik?"

"It's my ship." Five degrees up.

"This might cause problems for Anna."

"You like her too much."

"Edik."

"Fine!" Edik swore and leveled off as though this had been a small adjustment and nothing more. "Poll the others. And find out what *her highness* wants to do. But North doesn't set foot on my bridge."

30

Meditation was Carl's favorite way to pass time on local flights. A chance to center himself, gather his power, and let the deeper parts of his mind explore questions he had no time to consider consciously. Many times over the course of his career, his life had been saved by flashes of insight gained through meditation.

Besides, he had no desire to sit here and watch North drool over Anna, any more than he wanted to watch Anna and Edmund specifically avoid making googly eyes at each other.

And Oolaut, well, so far Oolaut hadn't proven to be much of a conversationalist.

The seats were comfortable, the temperature moderate, and his belly complaining that dinner was long past due. That hint of pomegranate smell in the air didn't help. Meditation was the ideal way to set all these minor irritations aside and bring himself back into focus. And that might be important by the time he met Oolaut's "people."

So the sudden appearance of Barshai's familiar, carrying news that Lukyanov was following them — which should have been obvious to anyone — was just one more unwelcome distraction.

"So what?" Carl said. "Let Lukyanov follow. What does Barshai want to do, fight him ship to ship?"

"No!" said Anna, who apparently missed Carl's attempt at irony. "The *Kiev* has—"

She cut herself off mid-sentence, clasping both hands over her mouth.

"Has what?" said Edmund, hand extended but not quite touching her arm.

"Military grade weapons," said North, as though it were the most obvious thing in the world. Which, frankly, Carl thought it was.

Anna's eyes grew so wide her eyeballs were at risk of falling out of their sockets.

"How did you—"

"This is Luna, and the *Kiev* is the private helioship of one of the major families," said Carl, with as much patience as he could muster, which meant his tone was a bit clipped. He could still hear Natalia Romanova imploring him to kill Alexei Lukyanov. "Of course they have military grade weapons and wards. They're not supposed to, but unless they get into a fight off-world, who would ever question it?"

Anna lowered her hands.

"We're hated," she said, voice small. But at least there were no tears in her eyes, and her jaw was firm. "Aren't we?"

"Yeah," said North, but even louder Carl said, "That's a question for another time. Right now Barshai wants our opinions about your father's ship, and I'm personally not of a mind to see us enter firing range."

Dola's head snapped left, those odd cerulean eyes focusing hard on Oolaut.

"Let me guess," said Carl, unfolding his legs and slipping his feet back into his loafers, "Oolaut doesn't want to cause us any trouble."

"Actually, he said that his people can defend themselves. They do not need us to fight their battles."

"Settles that then," said North. "Let's get this over with."

"Defend themselves how?" said Carl.

"He would prefer not to demonstrate," said Dola.

"No killing," said Edmund, which must have been the chorus of his favorite family song or something, as often as the kid said it. Even Duane would have stopped harping on this tune by now.

Anna nodded emphatic agreement.

"I guess that's it for our opinions then," said Carl. "We move ahead and let the chips fall where they may."

"No," said Anna.

Carl looked at her. So did everyone else, for that matter.

"No," she said again. "Father will try to exploit Oolaut's people, and he's used to getting his own way."

"He wouldn't try to strong-arm them," said Carl. "We're still talking about a first contact kind of situation."

"A what?" said Edmund.

"First contact," said North. "'s an old term, from back when people thought there were people on the other worlds, not just spirits."

Carl blinked in surprise that North knew even that much.

"He's right. The military still has regulations on the books about it, but people stopped expecting it to happen ten, maybe fifteen years ago."

"Father is ... accustomed to getting his way."

North grumbled something that he probably thought was amusing, but Edmund said something comforting to Anna at the same time, so Carl was spared hearing either.

And frankly, another party needed a voice in this discussion.

"Oolaut," said Carl, looking directly into those yellow eyes. Assuming they were eyes, and not actually its ears, or its sex organs — if a rock creature could have sex organs — or something else that Carl didn't even want to consider as a possibility. "Oolaut, those of us on this ship just want to get you home to your people. Maybe introduce ourselves. We mean you no harm. But others are following us. And we cannot guarantee their motives nor can we vouchsafe their behavior."

Carl glanced at Dola, to see if his words were getting through at all. Dola nodded encouragement, so Carl continued.

"You say you do not need us to fight for you. We appreciate that.

We don't want to fight if we don't have to. But our options are limited. We could take you straight home and ignore those who follow behind, knowing that they will see where we take you, or we could delay your return and try to prevent the others from following us. What would you have us do?"

Nothing.

No. Wait. Something. A tiny pulse of magic, not localized, but around Oolaut. Carl had spotted an aura around it before, a tight field of life/spirit/magic/whatever that surrounded its body the way larger ones surrounded humans and animals. But now, that pulse was like a brief violet flash through a clear, Barrier-yellow layer that couldn't have extended more than a centimeter or two from the creature's rocky flesh.

Carl looked at Dola.

"I don't know," said Dola. "It's never done that—" His feline ears twitched and his whiskers quivered. "No. Wait."

Dola looked at Carl, and those eyes looked troubled now.

"Oolaut says to let them follow. His people will be ready."

31

"Ignore them?" said Edik, sitting forward in his pilot's chair and thinking longingly of a ham-and-cheddar sandwich down in the galley — Lunar ham, unfortunately, which always had a chicory undercurrent that he didn't care for, but better than the nothing he'd had for too many hours. Alas, getting food would have meant feeding North too.

Hunger was the more appealing option.

So Edik let his stomach rumble as he regarded the *Kiev* on the scanners.

Like most modern helioships, the *Third Son* had two levels of accuracy for its scanners. The first was the basic level, a three-dimensional holographic illusion of the air or space around the ship, which focused in on any anomaly. Barshai's display was designed to be adjustable and tunable with one hand, so he could customize while flying in traffic.

But right now Edik had a hand on one of the two glowing green hand grips, which projected more detailed images directly into his mind and allowed a greater degree of flexibility, control, and precision. Two hands on the grips would have been better, but one hand was enough to let him have a good look at the *Kiev* floating, patient, above him.

To be precise, ten kilometers above him, and maybe six hundred meters behind.

"Just *let* them follow us in?"

"That's what the others say."

"They do understand that Lukyanov won't want to share this discovery with peons like us." Edik let go of the scanners grip and glanced out the bridge forward viewer — a fancy term for a part of the hull rendered transparent like a giant porthole — over the Lunar landscape. Small towns with correspondingly small Barriers, some private estates on the side of the occasional peak. Small pieces of habitability in the otherwise desolate land.

Any one of these places could have been a possible destination, as far as his pursuer were concerned. Edik could swoop low, pretend to land, then fly the rest of the way within a hundred meters of the rocky surface.

Dangerous, yes, but he could do it. And the others just wanted to let Lukyanov follow them.

Edik adjusted his trim and started angling back toward the Pillar.

"He's already got a death squad with him, and when he sees Oolaut and its people, he'll remove any pesky impediments to his getting credit in the history books. And take his daughter home in the process. That's just what men like him do."

"I'm pretty sure Carl Jones understands that. And Roger North had a resigned look in his eye, so he probably understands as well. Edmund McCutcheon is too wide-eyed to comprehend what's at risk. As for Anna, conflict roils within her. Difficult to say."

Edik gave his familiar a sidelong glance, then shrugged.

"This is a stupid thing to die over," he said.

"Weren't you just saying this morning that you expected to starve to death by next week?"

"Yes, but that would be the result of my own failure as a business-man. Much more appropriate than getting murdered so some rich bastard can claim credit for our discovery."

"You know," said Dola, "there's always a chance that this Lukyanov will be gracious and let you stay alive as a witness to his triumph."

"Do you believe that?"

"Not really, no."

"Right." Edik glanced at his readouts, the row of projected nearby sites of interest and distances above the white counters that housed the bridge portion of his ship's phantasmal workspace. Maybe ten minutes until they landed, if he held his current speed and course. "Think Akintola's flying right now? She likes night flights, and an impartial witness would sure help our chances of survival."

"She booked a Toronto run today. Doesn't expect to be back until tomorrow at the earliest, and that assumes—"

"That she doesn't take any local charters first for the excuse to see family. Crap." He swigged from a flask of lemon-flavored water. "Anybody else reliable you can think of?"

"No one who'd risk Lukyanov's wrath for us."

Edik blinked. He had an idea, but that was too crazy. Even for him. He swigged more water as he tried to talk himself out of it.

"Edik," said Dola, "we don't have time for any fancy maneuvers here. The others want to fly straight in. If you're that worried about Lukyanov, we could drop them off and—"

"Please, I haven't come this far to chicken out." He shoved the rest of his sandwich in his mouth, the sticky wheat bread impairing his words as he kept speaking. "'ut 'an 'and..."

He swallowed a couple of times, took another drink of water, and tried again.

"What can stand against a great family of Luna?"

"No, Edik," said Dola. "Calling in another great family is really not a good solution here."

"Not just any great family. The Romanovs. They'll be too busy trying to deny each other credit to—"

"This will never work."

"Sure it will. Have some faith."

Edik selected a strand of the glowing blue web. But before he could twist it, Dola said, "Edik, right now Lukyanov has no idea about Oolaut. He's just following his daughter. Or maybe he wants to see what we've discovered."

Edik stared, waiting for the big gray cat to come to the point.

"If we tell Natalia Romanova, she'll start maneuvering before we even touch down. And you think Lukyanov's got resources?"

"You're saying I'd be killing us faster than Lukyanov could?"

"I'm saying that Natalia Romanova could get the Lunar cops to believe we stole Oolaut from her grounds when you were there earlier today. I'm saying she'll have her story all ready, and you'll be executed by public hanging while she basks in whatever glory she could squeeze out of this."

Edik tried to find a hole in Dola's logic, but once again his familiar was ten steps ahead of him. But then, Edik had also forgotten about how Lunar capital crimes were punished...

"You can't read my mind at all, can you?" He said. "You're just smarter than I am."

"Well, that part goes without saying," said Dola. "Now, don't you think you should release that comm strand?"

"No. This is stupid." Edik let go of that strand, grabbed another, and twisted while with his other hand he brought his ship to a hovering halt.

In the air above the comm pad appeared a young, clean-shaven man's face. Square jaw, square nose, short black hair, and so pale he must never have left his ship and seen any actual sunlight.

Edik started speaking before the communications officer had the chance.

"*Kiev*, this is Captain Edik Barshai of the *Third Son*, just what the hell do you want?"

"You contacted us, *Third Son*. You tell me."

"Put your captain on, dimwit. Or better yet, Alexei Lukyanov."

"I cannot confirm or deny the presence of any member of the Lukyanov—"

"Put. Your. Captain. On."

"Not. Until. You tell me. Why."

Punching a comm image would accomplish nothing. No part of the movement would be transferred over the link. Even shouting only came across through tone, not volume, as a bound-in safety feature.

But Edik's fist clenched anyway.

Someone pounded on the bridge door. North's voice barely carried through it. "Why the hell have you stopped Barshai? What are you playing at?"

"Shut that idiot up," said Edik to Dola, in syllables only his familiar could understand. The great cat shifted through the door into the main cabin.

Edik turned back to the image of the officious little prick delaying him.

"Listen here," he said. "I'm sure you think you're clever. Hell, maybe you are, in some sense of the word. But you pay attention, and I mean you listen really fucking good, because I'm only going to tell you this once. Your ship is following me. You know it. I know it. Now put your goddamn captain on this line so we can talk about this, or by the many deaths of Rasputin I will make you all follow me to Earth to get what you want. Or maybe Mars. Hell, maybe I'll take a flight around Ganymede, I understand the first steps toward settlement are underway these days."

"One moment."

The face of the officious prick was replaced by the stately visage of Alexei Lukyanov.

"Much better," said Edik.

"I'd not realized the *Third Son* was a helioship. Must be expensive to maintain for local tours."

"Why, you want to make a donation to the Keep Barshai Flying Fund?"

"What's your game, Barshai? I get why Jones would spirit away my daughter. Even if I cut off her finances, she's still the most beautiful woman he could hope to find. But the rest of you don't add up. A helioship captain, an airship skipper, and ... what ... somebody's intern? What's really going on here?"

"I have no reason to tell you," said Edik, though he felt inwardly pleased that Lukyanov was polite enough to attribute North only his proper title.

"And I have no reason not to set the exact same course you happen to set. The skies out here are public property." Lukyanov pulled a frown as though to mock Edik, then dismissed it. "When Anna crashed my airship she dug something up, didn't she? Tell me what it is, and I might leave you alone."

"Fine. We found an artifact. A sarcophagus, in fact. Real, hard evidence that the ancient Egyptians had—"

"I have not insulted your intelligence, Captain Barshai. Pray, do not insult mine."

"Look. We found something. I admit it." After all, what's to admit when Lukyanov had figured that much out on his own. "But it's no big deal, really. Just a coded message. Jones seems to think it's got military implications, but me, I think it looks too old to be of interest to anyone other than a historian. Just another finding left over from the first settlers. Hardly anything to waste your fuel on."

"But enough to waste *your* fuel?"

Edik shrugged. "It's Jones' money. He wants me to carry him and his rock to some other site for comparison, what do I care?"

"Comparison to *what*..."

Lukyanov looked off to one side and Edik got a chill down his spine. Not a rock. He should never have said *rock*...

"The Pillar," said Lukyanov.

Edik couldn't stop himself from clenching his jaw. Stupid, stupid, stupid.

"Thank you, Captain Barshai, I think I shall meet you at the Pillar and see just what it is that our Mr. Jones believes he has found."

Lukyanov cut the link before Edik could get a word out.

Dola came back in through the door. "Well, they've calmed down. I think..." Dola sat in formal cat pose, head high and tail wrapped around his forepaws. "What did you do, Edik?"

Edik gave Dola a sickly smile.

32

"You goddamn idiot!" raged North.

The door to the cockpit was open now, and Carl was all that stood between North and Barshai killing each other. Carl stood in the doorway, sword in one hand, enchanted ceramic combat knife in the other. The sword pointed at North while the knife kept Barshai honest.

Dola sat over by Oolaut, presumably keeping the strange creature calm, while Anna had broken down in tears in her chair and Edmund crouched in front of her, trying to calm *her*.

Carl was past adrenaline now. He'd reached the calm point he'd trained for. For him, emotion and concerns had boiled away, leaving only simple, brutal practicality. His heart beat steady, strong, but slow. No sweat. No twitchy anticipation. Not even hunger. Only the calm.

The calm that left him aware of the precise distances between himself and everyone else on the ship. Aware of who he would kill first, how, and what move would lead to the next.

If he had to strike. If he chose to strike.

He could smell Barshai's ham-and-cheese sandwich on his breath over the herbs and borscht of the cockpit to his left, and the spring-fresh scent of the main cabin air.

Usually this state required intention. A mission. But he had it anyway, and no mental room to wonder if this was a good thing.

Two and one half threats present. The half currently appeared contained by the familiar. The other two seethed over. If needed, Carl could dispatch them both before they could draw their swords.

And chances were that North and Barshai knew it. That the weapons in Carl's hands kept those two captains from making any serious attempt to draw steel.

"Call me an idiot again, North," yelled Barshai. "I'll gut you here and now."

"Try it! Idiot!"

"Enough." Carl didn't yell. He didn't have to. In fact, in this state, he couldn't yell. Yelling took emotion. He could only make his voice carry.

And that one word rang out.

Both captains stared at him now. North spoke first.

"I'm getting mighty tired of—"

"Try to finish that sentence and you utter your last words."

"He's not kidding," said Dola, urgency in his tone, followed by words only Barshai could understand.

North turned and punched the headrest of the nearest passenger chair, snapping it off with a cushioned *whump*.

"You're gonna pay for that," started Barshai, but Carl interrupted.

"Silence."

Carl waited until he had their attention again before continuing.

"Keep your tallies. Mark your debts. Hate each other with all the passion you can muster. But do so in silence. If we come through this alive, then and only then you may kill one another, bill each other, or do whatever it is you need to do. But for now, for this one night, we are all on the same side. Can you accept this, or must I take your lives so that the remainder of us can present a united front?"

Carl didn't really know what he looked like in this state. He couldn't see the expression in his own eye, and he had no attention to spare for the details of his posture or bearing. But he remembered the first time he saw his former partner and mentor, Old Zachariah, in this state. He went from genial and funny to the essence of Death itself.

The most frightening thing Carl had ever seen.

So, in terms of pure practicality, Carl was not surprised at the looks of shock that surrounded him right now. The reassessments. The fear that would linger well past this one night.

A reason Carl's friends were few.

But more important was what he saw past their fear — acceptance. Even before either of them spoke, he knew what their answers would be.

Barshai spoke first, hands up as though to remind Carl that he was unarmed. "Sounds good to me. United front tonight. North and I can settle up tomorrow."

"Three days," said North, eyebrows high and hands spread wide. "Wasn't that what you said earlier, Jones? Three days we have to wait? Well, a good businessman like me understands the value of putting aside short-term interests when the long-term payouts are better. So, yeah, united front. Rah, rah team."

"I'm with you too," said Edmund, standing, jaw set despite the flutter in his knees. "We can do this."

Anna nodded, but at least she stopped crying. In Carl's current state, sympathy was an option he couldn't afford.

Carl sheathed his sword, exaggerating the motion to conceal where he replaced the combat knife in the same movement.

"Now," he said. "Lukyanov is on his way to the Pillar. There's no way to avoid his interference."

"He'll probably kill us," groused North, but then he gave Carl a calculating look. "Most of us, anyway."

"Then we may have no choice but to kill him first." Calculations coming together in Carl's mind. While killing Lukyanov had not been part of his intended plan, this might be for the best. On a purely practical level, Romanova would be a good associate to have, and the payout was considerable. "I'll handle the magician and Lukyanov himself. The rest of you focus on his guards."

Anna said something, but too soft for Carl to hear.

"We might have to face more than those six," said Barshai. "Blood starts spilling the rest of his crew might get into the mix."

"Not likely," said North. "The money man goes down, they'll lose their motivation to fight. No money in dying for a dead man."

Anna stood. Her stance was firm, chin high, hands balled into fists by her side.

"I said no."

33

THEY ALL STARED AT ANNA.

Carl, still standing in the cockpit doorway between Captains North and Barshai, putting away the weapons that were never far from his hands or his thoughts. Just looking at Carl would have been enough to speed her heart were it not already racing, but not because his features and build were handsome, nor because of the risk of his dangerous profession. Not in that moment.

It was the truth of the man she saw in Carl's eyes. So distant. So … absent of anything she recognized as human. Father had been right about him, to that extent at least. This man was a pure killer. The sight of him made her knees try to shake. A small voice deep within begged her to run. Run before he killed her. Before he killed everyone.

She might as well have been looking at a hungry bear.

But much as the man had shed his mask, Anna knew she had shed her own. Her tears were gone now. They might return later, someplace private, but they would not surface now.

For all the fear fluttering her stomach and racing her heart, for all the turmoil of loss and love and confusion, her spine held straight as truth, and not a speck of flush or perspiration would betray her poise.

Whatever else, she was a Lukyanova. Born to command.

Captain Barshai, just beyond Carl in the cockpit, stared at her in wonder.

Captain North, this side of Carl but still a good two meters in front of her, stared in desire that bordered on worship. It seemed the man had only two emotions, both of them base.

Edmund stepped back from her until he fell into the swiveling chair opposite her. But his eyes never wavered. Edmund, so full of good intentions but so sheltered in his own way as Anna had been in hers. Edmund stared in awe. She held up a hand to still him into silence. She knew where he stood and did not need his support for what she had to do next.

Edmund nodded, too quickly.

A small part of Anna hoped he would not be too cowed by her. A thought for later.

Just behind her to the right, she could hear Dola muttering something to Oolaut in a language she did not understand. Oolaut seemed to respond in scent, anise and holly, unless she was mistaken, over the spring air smells of the passenger cabin.

But Oolaut would wait. The men in front of her came first.

"Killing, killing, killing," said Anna. "Is that all you men can think about?"

Anna crossed her arms over her chest.

"You want to kill each other. You want to kill my father. My brother. Their men. Whoever tries to stop you from — what — doing the right thing? Returning lost Oolaut to his own people? Getting *credit* for it in the history books?"

She shook her head once, slowly.

"Well I tell you now, no, you will not. You will not kill them. You will not fight them. You will not even draw your weapons. If my father shows his face, *I* will speak with him and *I* will resolve this."

"A lovely thought," said Captain North, "but your daddy doesn't seem to hold you in what I'd call high esteem."

"I hate to agree with North," said Captain Barshai, "but he has a point. Lukyanov looked ready to turn you over his knee and send you to your room without any roast pheasant."

Carl said nothing.

"I understand how his words sounded to you. None of you know a man like Father—"

"I do," said Carl, his tone still flat. "I've known many like him."

"And he knows you, or so he says." She stepped straight up to Carl and looked him in those absent eyes. "Tell me, Carl Jones, are you nothing more than the killer my father says you are? Are you nothing but a weapon?"

That tiny voice inside Anna was panicked now, screaming in fear that never made it out of the back of her mind. Did not shatter her iron control.

But standing so close she could smell his summery male scent, so close he could snap her neck before she could move, she could feel the barest thread of a crack begin to spread through that control.

But she held herself straight. And she waited.

And suddenly, somebody was home.

It was like watching tea spread through a cup of hot water, the way humanity bled back into Carl's brown eyes.

"No," he said, voice tight and the sound almost raw. "I am not just a weapon."

"Then perhaps there's more to *him* than you think, too."

Anna turned away to give him space.

"And you." Anna stepped up to Captain North, challenging the lust in his eye. "Violence, greed and lust. That's all I've heard from you."

"What else is there?" he said with a smirk. "Don't try your—"

"Enough." She bored into him with her blue eyes. Saw something hiding there. Something tucked away, afraid to look back. And Captain North blinked like he knew she saw it, but he shoved his jaw forward as she continued. "If that's all you are, fine. Your lust will get no relief from me. Keep it to yourself. And I don't care whether your fill your purse or not. But until Oolaut is safely home, you'll keep that sword sheathed until *I* tell you to draw."

Captain North leaned closer. She could smell cashews and bourbon on his breath. He leaned closer still until they were nose to nose.

"Is that right?" he said.

"That's right." She did not yield a fraction.

North stared back, but he blinked first.

"Fine," said North, turning and throwing himself down on the chair he'd knocked the headrest off of. It creaked a loud complaint and spun him away from her. "Whatever, your *highness*."

Anna ignored the slight and turned to Captain Barshai.

"This is my ship," he said, "and you aren't paying the fare. I don't take orders from you, and you aren't going to shame me into anything."

Dola said something, but Anna couldn't understand it.

"Well, Captain Barshai, then it seems to me that you have a decision to make." She marched up to him, her riding boots and pants lending a military crispness to her steps. "Since this is your ship, do you want to throw it away on a fight you'll lose? Or do you want to listen to reason?"

"We might not lose," he said.

"You can only lose." She held up her left hand. "One possibility, Father and his men cut the lot of you to ribbons, and you get no glory, no money, just death." She held up her right hand. "The other, Carl leads you to victory. Then you will have murdered members of one of the great families of Luna."

Anna made a show of looking around the cabin, tracing the gold and red of the fixtures and furnishings with her eyes. "This is a helioship. You could run to Earth. To Mars. Perhaps even to Venus."

She looked back at him. "Of course, my family has many friends in business and politics on Earth ... Mars ..." She smiled. "Perhaps even Venus. No matter where you ran, you would be caught and punished brutally."

Captain Barshai bit his lip and looked past her to Dola.

But Anna wasn't done.

"You call your ship the *Third Son*." She pointed to the great red feather mural painted the length of the cabin ceiling. "Your ship is shaped like a firebird. So ask yourself. What would Ivan Tsarevich do, in your place?"

Captain Barshai's jaw dropped.

"No one has ever gotten the reference before."

"If you run in circles where no one recognizes references to the greatest hero in all Russian folk tales, you need new friends." She fluttered her eyelashes. "Well? What would he do?"

"He would save Oolaut." Captain Barshai shook his head and sighed. "Fine, we'll play it your way, but..."

"Yes?" she prompted. Captain Barshai's eyes widened as slowly as a smile spread across his face.

"But *Ivan Tsarevich would call the right allies.*"

34

EDIK TURNED AND JUMPED INTO HIS PILOT'S CHAIR, HEART PUMPING with excitement at being compared to Ivan Tsarevich, even in mocking tones.

How many stories had his father told of Ivan Tsarevich? Ivan and the Gray Wolf. The Apples of Rejuvenation. The Sea Tsar. Even putting an end to Koschei the Deathless. Ivan Tsarevich was the boyhood hero Edik had told himself he'd outgrown.

But now? Escorting this Oolaut home while opposing a corrupt noble? This could be Edik standing in for Ivan in a new tale. Perhaps *Ivan Tsarevich and the Stone Hound*. Or maybe Oolaut was more like a lizard. No. Edik liked "stone hound" better.

His eyes checked the readouts while his chair creaked and rocked back into position. With one hand Edik absently brushed crumbs from his sandwich off of the white ceramic display counters.

"See why I like her?" said Dola, padding in to stand beside him. "I told you she was smart."

But Edik's eyes were on the display. The *Kiev* was ahead of him now, but still flying way up above. Nothing else in the skies near him, and more importantly nothing else flying around the Pillar.

Ten minutes out, unless he pushed his speed and drew the interest of everyone with a scanner on this side of Luna.

That would be going too far.

"Would you like control back, Edik?" said Nixia, swirling back into her meter-tall yellow seeming and drawing a startled "ooh" of appreciation from Anna Lukyanova, barely two steps behind him.

So, for all her airs and mockery she *was* still a teenage girl. Edik had started to wonder.

"Not yet, thank you," he said to Nixia. "Keep the course steady and let me know if the others pick up anything unexpected."

"Of course," she said, swirling back into invisibility, spreading herself out to work directly with the other air elementals of the planetary drive.

Dola made a small sound of hesitations as Edik hooked a finger into a glowing blue strand above his communications pad.

"Edik," said Dola in words only they could understand, "are you sure?"

Edik drew a deep breath, smiled at the lingering smell of borscht, nodded, and started to pinch the connection.

But North interrupted him.

"Just a damn minute, Barshai. We got a right to know who you're calling."

"Much as I hate to agree with him," said Anna, "he has a point."

"He's calling the news," said Jones.

Edik let go of the strand and looked at Jones, not trying to hide the shock on his face.

"Stands to reason," said Jones. "You want credit. You want a chance at the money that might come in from this. You want to keep Lukyanov from stealing either, and you still want to get Oolaut home."

"That ... hadn't even occurred to me," said Edik with a grin. "But my idea's better. I'm calling Kennedy Thaum."

North's turn to grin.

"Talk to Jakes," he said with a wink, "in the Lunar Studies branch. I've dealt with him before."

"No!" Edik couldn't keep the sharpness out of his tone. Yes, Edik had been ready to make just such a deal earlier. Not to hurt Oolaut, but only to keep food in his belly a roof over his head and a place to dock his ship.

Still, Ivan Tsarevich would never have offered Oolaut to the university for study. Not even if it meant giving up his last crust of bread.

But maybe, just maybe, there was a way to do the right thing and still come out ahead. After all, an evening of playing Ivan Tsarevich wouldn't keep the wolf — or his creditors — from his door.

"Why?" said Anna Lukyanova. "What's wrong with this Professor Jakes?"

"Not a prof," said North. "He's a grad student, struggling same as us poor pilots. Not all of us grew up on fancy estates with our own Barriers, you know."

"Calling a graduate student," said Edmund, somewhere behind Jones, "about something this big? Sounds underhanded to me."

"Me too," said Anna Lukyanova.

"Look," said Edik. "Everybody calm down. We're not trying anything tricky here. No, North, we're not. North knows Jakes, and Jakes can get us in touch with someone who has actual authority."

"Plus," said North, rallying with a bit too much enthusiasm, "Jakes has his own runabout. I've worked with him before. He's sure to get there, maybe faster than this bucket of clay and sticks." North edged forward, giving Jones and Anna Lukyanova as much space as he could. "I can make direct contact. Let me link him."

"Good luck with that," said Edik, holding up his left hand. "This is the best you get. I handle the link, you handle connection."

North snarled, but snatched Edik's left hand with his right, squeezing a good deal harder than was thaumaturgically necessary to bridge the connection.

But Edik felt North work the magic right, at least, and the intention flowed through Edik. So guided, he selected just the right spot on just the proper strand of his blue communications web, and pinched.

Jakes had skin the color of teak, and a burn scar from some sort of alchemical accident spattering his left cheek. Dark brown eyes and thick dreadlocks. He looked more like someone who dressed scenes for shadow plays than a serious academic.

Edik tasted sour suspicion and glanced sideways at North who was smiling like Jakes was his best friend in the world.

That alone was suspicious. Who'd befriend a fare-stealing bastard like North?

"That you North?"

"It's me," North said, grin in his voice and on his face. "The sky rat next to me is Barshai."

Jakes' eyebrows came up. "You're working with the Barshai? Since when?"

"Since we found something today that you want a piece of. Trust me."

"Not just you," said Edik quickly. "Get your department head or we skip you and go straight to the news."

"You call me you get me," said Jakes. "You want Professor Funkuro, call him. His office hours start at thirteen hundred tomorrow."

"Ease down that throttle," said North, crouching for eye level with Jakes. "Have I ever steered you wrong?"

Jakes narrowed his eyes.

"All right," said North with a laugh, "have I ever steered you away from money?"

Jakes gave a grudging nod.

"And North's the reason we're calling you," said Edik. "But here's the thing. This has all, every part of it, got to be done to code. Nothing tucked in a hold."

"What he means," said North, giving Barshai a sour look for dropping into pilot jargon when dealing with an academic, "is there's nothing black market to any of this. There can't be or" — North grimaced — "or you're out. And likely so am I."

"This better be big."

"Get your department head," said Edik, "get your tools, and get to the Pillar lacuna-fast."

And then Edik told him why.

35

CARL SPENT THE REST OF THE FLIGHT AT THE BACK OF THE MAIN CABIN. Let the others sit near the cockpit, edging forward with excitement. Anna with her noble aspirations. North with his greed. Edmund...

Carl wasn't sure about Edmund. A desire to do the right thing, perhaps. Or just an interest in Anna. Carl couldn't blame him for that, especially after her show of strength.

Mid-cabin Oolaut perched on a chair made for lounging, stone head craning this way and that, observing and studying according to its own alien reasoning.

Barshai and his familiar, of course, in the cockpit.

Here at the back of the cabin, Carl could find a moment of peace. Could sink deeper into his meditations. Meditations for his power, yes, and to organize his mind for his magic — which he was sure to need before all this ended. But he needed meditation for more than that right now.

Carl had to get his head straight.

First, he had to set aside his hunger. Nothing but those few apple slices in his stomach since Zira's. He had fought a duel since then, and come close to spilling blood several more times.

Food would be best right now. Red meat. Fibrous vegetables.

Bread that came in hunks. Water or beer to wash it down. But none of that was in the offering.

So Carl withdrew deeper into himself. Past the sensations of his body. And more importantly, past the questions in his mind. Questions he'd ignored for years until Anna stabbed straight to their heart with disturbing accuracy.

Carl had trained for years to serve. To turn all the talents of his body and mind to helping the whole of humanity. Spying on the colonies for Earth. Spying on the corporations that thought they were above the law.

Killing when he had to.

But what had he become? What was he now? No cause to serve, no goals to guide him. Only the skills he'd gained. Only the fat offers from the corporations to serve *their* good instead. Improve their security, fighting the men and women who still did what Carl used to do.

Spying on one corporation for another.

Carl could not. Would not.

And so he became a licensed champion. A profession with some respect and glamour, and for which he was most suited.

And yet, as Anna Lukyanova had so unerringly pointed out, nothing more than a weapon. As he had been for years.

So who was Carl? What was he really?

He did not know. And he knew he could not afford to indulge such existential questions. He had a mission. One he had given himself, for the first time. To get Oolaut home safely, no matter who or what stood in his way.

It might be the single finest thing Carl had ever done.

And he was not going to fuck it up now by getting lost in questions of purpose and meaning.

So Carl pushed his mind past those questions. Past the tightness in his muscles, clenching to defend against unwanted thoughts.

Ease those muscles back. Ease those muscles until slack. Feet. Calves. Thighs. Buttocks. Groin. Abdomen. Torso. Shoulders. Arms. Forearms. Hands. Neck. Jaws. Eyes. Scalp.

One by one Carl focused his attention on each muscle group in his body, moving upward, feeling every bit of tension within it and easing that tension out. Leaving behind only a warm relaxation.

One by one, every stressor dismissed or shelved for later. One by one, every fret or concern ebbed away from him, until Carl sat, cross-legged in the passenger chair, hands on his knees.

Balanced. Relaxed. Calm. His heart rate slow. His breathing slower still, and deep as space itself.

The routine of practice drew Carl's mind to notice and dismiss every active spell and enchantment around him, starting with his own ceramic combat knife and spiraling out into the ship. Every spell-hardened bit of hull. Every line of wards, bonds, circles, and containments necessary to take this great hunk of fired clay and carterite and transform it into a helioship, capable of safely traveling the millions of kilometers between planets.

Carl could feel the earth elementals providing heat and comfort. The water elementals from the water closet behind him. The air elementals freshening the air as well as carrying the ship through the skies and detecting everything around it.

The dormant lacuna of the ship's space drive, that space elemental that carried the ship between planets.

And within the ship. Dola on the bridge. Barshai's familiar. Anna's mourning bracelet? That might merit a question or two later. North carried a veracitor in one pocket, a small lens that could detect lies.

Of course a man like North carried a veracitor. That they were illegal in business dealings on Luna would not deter him. Not when much of his business was likely illegal.

Finally, there was Oolaut itself. The Barrier-yellow aura, not a coincidence. A spark of life within that Barrier, perhaps held in place by...

Could it be?

Carl had to hold back. Could not risk probing at Oolaut. He had no way to know what Oolaut could detect of human magic, and worse than that, what Oolaut might take offense to. Carl had to settle for only the gentlest of probes. Looking, not staring.

And yet.

Carl had been thinking of that personal Barrier as an aura, as all living things have auras. But rock. How could anything create true life out of rock itself? It didn't seem possible.

So what if it was something else? What if Oolaut was a spirit in its natural state, but was able to enter and animate the rock it now occupied?

That should not have been possible either. Not as far as Carl knew. Though it did sound more plausible than sparking life in something that could not breathe, could not bleed. Also, admittedly, Carl's thaumaturgic education was more than a smidgeon limited, and it covered little beyond the skills he needed for his work.

But Carl did have his field experience, and while he had seen a few animated statues, they had been very few. Created only by Hierophants, and Carl had been given to understand that the spells and alchemy involved in creating and maintaining such automata were demanding and costly.

Carl could detect no spells on the rock that made up Oolaut's body. No bindings or wards. No scent of alchemy, save for ginger, bay leaves, and alkaline, which made sense since the greenish rock of Oolaut's body seemed formed from the Failed Site.

So it didn't seem like life. But it didn't seem like an automaton either, not like any Carl had ever seen. And that tight aura, an unchanging Barrier yellow. That had to mean something too. But what?

No. That question was a distraction too.

Carl sank deeper into his meditations, preparing himself for whatever would happen when they landed.

Carl could not worry about what Oolaut was. Let that Professor Funkuro determine that.

As long as the determination did not stop Oolaut from getting home safely.

Otherwise, Carl might have to kill him.

36

Edik took the *Third Son's* controls in his own hands as the time grew near to land at the Pillar. With an approach vector that would satisfy anyone with both a scanner and an overdeveloped sense of curiosity, Edik let Nixia give the "strap in" warning and opened up the throttle.

Tongue forward, between his teeth as he flew by sight and instinct more than trusting his readouts now. He had that good tension in his gut and in his shoulders. His knees spread as he leaned into the movement, as though he flew without any ship at all.

His heels bounced in time to an internal rhythm.

Down and down he went.

He could see the curve of the incline up the crater now. The grayish white and blueish white rock of the moon's surface showing through past the thinning grass and brownish dirt around the groves of pine and spruce and fir. All oddly lit by the dark yellow glow of the Barrier.

Toward the Pillar itself.

Just inside of the crater's edge it stood. Two kilometers tall, half a kilometer thick at the base and tapering the whole way up in a gradual spiral. Greenish yellow, and just the sight of it again brought the memory of its stench: sour rum and coconut, mostly, but also peony and coriander.

Edik's stomach complained at the memory, as though it were a bad hangover. Honestly, Edik always felt a little hungover when he left the Pillar. And the tourists he'd taken there often said the height of it made them dizzy.

But that always passed quickly.

The best part about the location of the Pillar was that a ship the size of the *Kiev* couldn't land nearly as close as the *Third Son* could. Speaking of the *Kiev*, Edik glanced over at the scanners.

"Hah!" Edik allowed himself a small chortle as he pointed Dola to the scanners. The *Kiev* might have reached the sky above the Pillar first, but they'd been unwilling to dip below the ten kilometer mark until then.

And without anywhere clean to land, Edik had all the edge.

Maybe they wouldn't need North's friends from the university anyway. Maybe they'd be able to drop off Oolaut and kiss sky again before Lukyanov even found out what happened.

Except that the *Kiev* was dropping faster now. They must have seen a good landing spot.

Another ship on the scanners now. Coming from Kennedy. Smaller. Runabout class. Had to be the academics. This might turn into a—

"Edik!" cried Dola.

Edik glanced back out the viewer, expecting another ship. Expecting a tall tree maybe, or some peak he'd ignored. His hands ready to steer around as needed.

Instead he saw *them*.

Hundreds of them. Creatures like Oolaut, only not from greenish rock. All bluish white or grayish white. And hard to tell from here, but they didn't look nearly so thick as Oolaut did either. Thinner. Longer.

All of them crowded around in the largest clearing, just short of the Pillar.

And every one of them looking straight up at the *Third Son*. Every.
Single. One.

"Dola," said Edik, easing back on the throttle, "maybe you better
go talk to Oolaut and make sure we're not walking into a disaster."

Dola ran straight through the closed door, into the main cabin.

"Nixia!" he shouted. Edik's heart was racing now, and the tension
in his gut and shoulders had spread down his legs and arms. Only
years of practice had kept his hands from clenching when he needed
them supple.

That clearing would have been perfect for the *Third Son*, plenty
big and plenty close without the threat of bumping into the oddest
natural feature on Luna.

"Edik?" she said, wise enough to pull herself together into her
feminine yellow form *beside* him instead of in front as usual.

"I need to land and I need to land now. And I don't want to do
anything to scare or upset the natives."

"Natives? *Oh.* Like Oolaut."

"Can you all— Never mind. I need your help guiding in."

"I could run ahead and talk to them."

"No time. I need you to—"

"Were you aware that the *Kiev* is coming down almost on top
of us?"

"What!" Edik spared a glance from his frantic search of the
ground. Sure enough the *Kiev* was coming down nearly as fast as he
was, and it didn't look as though they cared where they landed.

Edik's comm pad flashed red. Then orange. Two links, both trying
to reach him right now.

"Dola!" he shouted, forcing himself to maintain speed that might
end his little trip real quick. To Nixia he said, "Help me, Nix, please.
Anywhere we can set down without crashing, close to the crowd as
possible and still stay safe."

Nixia slid into the phantasmal workspace, a warm, fluttery sensa-
tion across his aura that felt better than he wanted to think about.
Dola had a point about Edik needing a date. But she could receive

and process information from the ship's other elementals faster than even the workspace could.

"Edik?" said Dola, coming back through, but needed no more words to see the orange flashes of the comm pad.

"You have reached the *Third Son*," said Dola, opening a link to whichever had priority according to protocol, "but Captain Edik Barshai is otherwise engaged. What message may I deliver?"

"Barshai," said the loud voice of Alexei Lukyanov, "you have one of those things on your ship, don't you? Cut a deal with me here and now, Barshai, and I'll see to it you're set for life."

A small voice inside Edik wondered just how much he could accomplish if he didn't have to worry about where his next meal was coming from. He wouldn't have to hustle for fares. Fight off jackals like North, for scraps. Upgrade the *Third Son*. Travel anywhere he wanted...

"Ivan Tsarevich cannot be bought!" he yelled.

There! A place where two groves of firs never grew together as had been planned.

No. It wouldn't work. There couldn't have been more than eight meters between them.

"Eight point three seven five," corrected Nixia, who knew what he saw.

"We need nine for landing and takeoff. We could never—"

"Come in from the front," said Nixia. "And trust me."

Edik nodded, his gut twisting at the words of his old professors. *Bound spirits were untrustworthy. Contain and constrain them at all time. Give them specific orders, or the slack you give them may shape the noose that hangs you.*

But Dola had been telling Edik something earlier. Something about the difference between himself and other magicians.

And with that huge fucking *Kiev* coming down almost on top of him, what choice did he have?

Edik angled the *Third Son* to come in along a vector that would set him down just between the two groves. All healthy, strong trees with thick, healthy trunks. The branches would hardly scuff the paint on the firebird wings, but those trunks. Even one, on only one side, might snap the tip of the wing.

Kennedy was a long hike away on foot. If Edik even lived to take the walk.

But he gritted his teeth and trusted Nixia while he heard Dola break the one link and open the other.

"*Third Son*," said a woman's voice, sultry, rich, and accustomed to getting what she wanted, "this is Natalia Romanova. I understand you've found something interesting."

37

ANNA WAS GRIPPING THE ARMRESTS OF HER CUSHIONED SWIVEL SEAT. Something was wrong. Something was very wrong, and she couldn't understand it.

Eight huge portholes in the main cabin of the *Third Son*, one in front of each seat, four on either side of the center aisle.

Anna had an excellent view as the ship dove and banked and twisted. She'd flown airships before — even without crashing — and she'd ridden in them hundreds of times. Maneuvers like this one should have had her careening into the five-point safety belt. She should have felt every twist and turn, once the pilot started getting fancy.

And yet, she sat as at ease and comfortable in her chair as though they flew straight through smooth skies.

Weirder still, Oolaut had started giving off another scent. Coconuts and something sour, but she wasn't sure what.

Captain North looked just as uncomfortable as she felt. His cheek dented as though he bit his own mouth for reassurance. His eyes narrowed and drops of sweat running down his forehead.

Anna contented herself with gripping the armrests.

"What does this mean?" she said. And when Captain North

looked at her blankly, she explained, "Why do we not feel this movement? Is there something wrong in the ship somewhere?"

"*Wrong?*" Abject shock all over that scruffy face, from the tip of his scraggly black beard to the scalp-high scraggly black eyebrows. "He's got the best damp'ner spells I've ever seen in a tour ship. No wonder I never snag any of his fares once they've kissed sky in this ship."

And yet, Captain Barshai had sounded on the brink of destitution. Anna had even considered offering to buy the *Third Son* in case he wanted to find another line of work.

How could—

Dola came through the cockpit door without opening it, his meter-tall gray bulk merely phasing through as though it were empty air.

Dimi's familiar went through doors that way. Orya, the most adorable semitransparent black bear she could imagine. Anna remembered the time Dimi had sent Orya through her door to wake her up on her tenth birthday, the bear rolling summersaults while juggling an imaginary ball with its feet.

Anna found herself smiling and her grip on the armrests easing when Dola halted in front of her.

"Anna Lukyanova, your presence is strongly requested on the bridge."

"Me?" Anna looked out the window. The *Third Son* sped toward the ground at a forty-five degree angle, looking for all the world as though Captain Barshai intended to crash into a small forest of firs. "What can I—"

"Please, Anna Lukyanova. The matter is urgent."

"Of course," she said, undoing her safety belts and standing.

"I'm coming too," said Captain North, already out of his safety belts, and Edmund nodded and began work on his. Carl remained where he had been most of the flight — sitting alone in the back of the cabin, meditating.

"Only Anna Lukyanova is requested. If the rest of you would—"

Captain North barged past and Anna had to hurry to keep up,

Dola and Edmund right on her heels. Captain North got the door open first.

"Huh?" he said, and he did not resist when Anna shoved him aside to step past and ... into the cockpit? Onto the bridge? She wasn't sure what the right phrase was.

And then she saw what made Captain North stop short.

Hovering above the *Third Son's* communications pad she saw the face of Natalia Romanova. Beautiful and distant, the perfect picture of old Russian nobility. Long hair the color of fine gold, curling in just a little at the bottom. High cheekbones, sharp jaw and chin. Aristocratic nose, and pale, pale blue eyes.

Compared to Natalia Romanova, Anna looked wretched, she was certain. But a Lukyanova did not bow her head. Not even though rumors had named Natalia Romanova an old lover of Father's. A rumor that came back to mind every time Anna saw that little smile on those rose-pink lips.

Natalia dropped immediately into Russian and Anna followed her.

"Anya, so good to see you. And so clever of you to leap ahead of both your father and me in this little race."

"Aunt Natya," — as Natalia insisted Anna call her — "I am pleased to see you as always, of course, but I do not understand. What race? What do you mean?"

"Droll as ever," Natalia replied with the perfect noble laugh, just the right amount of real humor mixed with a touch of superiority and a dash of intimacy, inviting the listener to trust.

Oh, if only Anna could laugh like that. But Natalia was still talking.

"But, my dear little Anya, this is not the time for games. You and your little friends have discovered something important. You and I must discuss what is to be done with it, and how and when we tell the rest of Luna."

"But, Aunt Natya, how—"

"Dear child, did your father never tell you? The Romanov family donates more to the universities of Luna than all the other great families combined. It is a point of pride for us that we are building a stronger Luna. A Luna that will one day stand beside Earth as an equal, and not only a colony."

So Professor Fukuro contacted her.

But that meant her knowledge was second hand...

"Oh, dear Aunt Natya," said Anna with a laugh of her own that, alas, paled beside Natalia's. "What stories you must have heard. I was only just lecturing my servants here about the dangers of telling tales. But what can one do, when one's pilot so loves his stories that he names his ship after Ivan Tsarevich?"

"Does he?" Polite. And unconvinced.

"Of course. The *Third Son* and shaped like a firebird."

"That ship was at my estate only today. He is not your private pilot, Anya."

"Of course not!" And for the first time in her life, Anna gave Natalia Romanova a patronizing smile and hoped that Natalia couldn't see the way her pulse leapt in her throat. "What would Father say if he found out I kept a pilot on retainer?"

"He would think you intended to run away, as you appear to have done, naughty girl."

"Father cannot control me, any more than old Boris Romanov could control you, my dear Aunt Natya. I am only following your marvelous example. But the most wonderful thing happened today. I wanted to wait until I could tell you in person but" — Anna laughed — "since you have already heard a far more wondrous tale than the truth, I shall have to settle for telling you now."

"We're coming in," said Captain Barshai, voice tight. Out of the corner of her eye, Anna could see the ship arrowing down, aiming for a break between those small forests of firs.

Edmund and Captain North ran back to their chairs and strapped in.

Anna merely drew breath and kept going, hoping for the best.

A trickle of sweat worked its way down between her shoulder blades.

"We found a statue at the Failed Site. Like a cross between a dog and a great lizard, and such tests as I could perform with the limited alchemical supplies I had on hand suggest it dates back thirty-five years or more. Before humans ever set foot on Luna, but after the rise of magic. Think of it Aunt Natya, hard evidence of nonhuman sentient life! And I discovered it!"

"But if *this* is true, where are its creators? Surely if such creatures existed, we would have found them here by now."

"A great deal of Luna's surface remains unexplored." Anna leaned closer, hushing her words. "That was why I contacted the university first. I wanted to see if they had discovered anything even remotely like what I have found."

Anna sighed.

"And here I must confess my great failing. I indulge my servants. One swore he had just the right confidential contact at the university to give me the information I needed, and another insisted — insisted to *me*, if you can believe it — that the statue bore some resemblance to the Pillar, and begged me to come see."

Anna smiled. "A fool's errand, of course, but it does save me from setting foot into the musty office of a career academic."

"Oh, Anya," said Natalia. "Dear, sweet Anya. I cannot number the times I have wished for a daughter with such beauty and grace as you possess."

Natalia leaned a little closer, that small smile again which reminding Anna that some might believe Natalia Romanova *was* her mother, despite the obvious way Anna's build resembled her real mother's.

"But, sweet Anya, you could not begin to lie to me."

38

"She ever going back to her seat?" muttered Edik, glancing back over his shoulder at Anna Lukyanova, who appeared to be having the time of her life while standing on *his* bridge and talking to Natalia Romanova through a link.

Smiling. Waving her hands. Streaming out her words in Russian that sounded beautiful, but was far too fast and smooth for Edik to follow. As though a conversation with the most powerful woman on Luna were an everyday pleasure.

Perhaps for Anna Lukyanova it was.

But Edik couldn't spare the women or the conversation more than a glance.

He had a ship to land, and not enough space to do it.

Hands on the controls, Edik guided the ship through a dive. A tricky dive, following the curve of the crater's incline, as close to the grayish, whitish rocks below, but not so close he threatened the crowd of ... whatever Oolaut's people called themselves.

And still he had to land just beyond the huge gathering of rocky, four legged incarnate spirits — every one of whom stared at his ship with those unsettling, flat, yellow eyes. Just like Oolaut's.

Nixia better be right about this.

Crashing wasn't a good option for anyone.

Nixia was gone now, and Edik's hands felt cold in her absence, one handling the throttle while the other danced from pitch lever to roll knob and back, dipping the nose then leveling off. Wings up on one side to center just a little better, then back to account for the wind.

And the wind blew rough out here. Rough enough that he had to spare attention for the yaw knob as well. Twisting the *Third Son* back on track every other gust.

Too much.

"Damn this wind!"

Edik slapped the white ceramic shelf in the right spot, signaling the phantom workstation to shift to combat controls — pitch, roll and yaw all now blended into one hypersensitive flight stick, with throttle control a tiny lever on the tip.

Edik hated this thing. He was no combat pilot.

"Nixia? I could use a hand here."

Nothing. She was busy handling … whatever she was handling.

Edik gripped the flight stick in both hands. Teeth clenched and jagged breaths flaring his nostrils. Shoulders tight as a hatch seal. Heels bouncing nonstop to the rapid pound of his heart.

Lower.

No more than a hundred meters up now. Ease back the throttle.

Too much! Too low too soon!

Pull back on the flight stick. Nose up. Bend right. Twist a hair.

Trees ahead looming. So big. Solid wall of wood.

Anna Lukyanova said something. To him. No time.

"Get back and strap in!"

Roar above him. The *Kiev* racing down.

Coming at him!

Edik banked hard to starboard. Kicking up the throttle and diving lower.

Too hard! The crater's edge came at him at speed.

Back on the stick. He pulled up, edging along the rocky surface. Landing approach gone.

"Dola! Where is it?"

Edik didn't know where his familiar had been, but now he was at the scanners. "The *Kiev* is going for the clearing just past the spruces. It'll rip out trees, but it'll land."

No time to circle up. Had to get back on track. Now.

Edik yanked back hard on the stick, banking even harder to port. The *Third Son* flew upside down now, and Edik had too damn good a look at the hundreds of rock creatures. All watching with no apparent concern.

Edik prayed.

He rolled the *Third Son* again, dropping his speed and diving. Twisting. Banking. Fighting the wind with his will as much as his flight stick.

Chosen landing spot coming fast.

Trees on both sides all too near.

"Nixia." Edik drew the name out.

He had the right angle. He hemorrhaged speed. And his arms shook as he fought the wind for that magic spot. At the edge of the clearing. Just inside the forest. On a path not quite wide enough for his ship's wingspan.

"*Now!*" Nixia's voice. A whisper in his ear.

Experience said she was wrong. Experience said too soon for the landing. Ship was too high yet.

Edik locked his right arm, holding his approach as steady as he could with a single hand.

He held his breath and closed his eyes.

Edik slapped the talons release, letting the firebird ship's legs extend and reach for the ground.

39

C<small>ARL WAS AIRBORNE</small>.

One moment he sat deep in meditation, running his mind through thaumaturgic exercises he'd begun learning in high school and extended through his military and governmental training.

The next moment, his eyes were open and his body was flying out of his seat. In the air above golden carpet with red trim. Legs still crossed. Every muscle loose and relaxed.

Training preceded thought.

Carl's neck tucked. His legs extended. His right arm shot forward, elbow bent just so. Left arm just behind it. Left hand behind right.

A perfect somersault. Carl finished standing, feet apart and balanced, knees bent and center of gravity low, ceramic combat knife in one hand and stiletto in the other.

And not a single enemy to fight.

Carl blinked. Shook his head.

Oolaut was safe, its pointed serpentine head tilted. Almost quizzical as it regarded him. And it smelled like sour rum and coconut, though Carl would have sworn that earlier it smelled like the Failed Site. Anna huddled into her seat, eyes closed tight and a white-knuckled grip on her armrests. Edmund the same, opposite, with his lips moving in nonstop prayer.

And beyond them both, North going through every cuss word he knew and probably making a few up. His posture angry and forward in his seat.

"What happened?" said Carl, sheathing his apparently unneeded weapons.

"*Impossible!*" North threw open the catches on his safety belts with disgust. He jumped to his feet. "Absolutely impossible."

"What is?"

Anna and Edmund both risked opening their eyes, and immediately stared in shock at North, who was raving now, hands flung out wide and more cuss words flowing freely.

Carl looked at Anna and Edmund, but they didn't seem to know what had the airship captain so upset.

Carl looked out the portholes on both sides of the ship. They appeared to be sitting on the ground, ensconced between thick-grown spruce trees on either side.

"Looks like an excellent place to land to me," said Carl, carefully, when North paused for breath.

North sneered with half his face, one eyebrow up. But whatever he intended to say shifted when the cockpit door opened.

"Well," said Barshai, actually dusting his hands as he strode in, smiling, with Dola marching tail high right behind him, "I'd say—"

"*What the hell did you do, Barshai?*" thundered North.

"Why, I landed my ship," said Barshai with mock innocence.

"*You pulled your wings in before landing!*" North was red-faced now, spit flying with every word. "Impossible. Violates every. Gonna report. I'll—"

Carl stepped over and slapped him hard, staggering the large man a step.

"That's enough. We don't have time for this. Whatever he did, he landed us safely. And I'm guessing it wasn't easy."

"Couldn't have done it without Nixia," said Barshai with a grin, and suddenly the air elemental swirled into existence in front of them all and bowed, the tiny image of feminine grace and beauty in pale yellow. "Finest air elemental I could hope to work with."

Questions furrowed Carl's brow. Barshai was talking about an elemental like a crew member. Carl had never seen that before. Never heard of anything like it. North must not have either, because he grumbled and shook his head, and Carl could make out the word "crazy."

But this was no time for questions.

"Well, however this works, thank you Barshai. And Nixia. And Dola, I presume." Dola raised his head to stand a little taller. "But right now, we need to get moving."

"Yes we do," said Dola. "The *Kiev* is on the ground, and I lost track of that runabout during the landing."

Dola trotted over to Oolaut, who jumped down and stepped forward. Smooth. Adroit. Not at all the timid, almost clumsy thing it had appeared to be earlier. Same thickness to the legs, "torso" and "head." Same dark yellow Barrier-color to the eye spots.

And yet the legs were definitely moving with more ease and confidence. Was it just glad to be home?

"We're here, Oolaut," said Anna, and Dola translated.

Barshai opened the hatch and Edmund went over to assist Anna — or just to stand near her — so Carl stepped in close to North.

"Are we going to have a problem?"

"Not unless you hit me again. I'll report Barshai later. *Major* safety violation. Don't know how he got it past inspection. Flying a ship that can—"

"I'm talking about your 'friend.' Jakes."

"Jakes?" North shook his head. "He fucked me when he fucked us all."

Anna and Oolaut moved past then, while North told Carl what he'd missed while he was meditating.

Carl ran his mind through his Lunar contacts, but it was too late to worry about that now. Maybe if someone had roused him when there was a problem...

No. Not this kind of problem. Not here, where family name meant more than any other affiliation.

"Come on," he said, trotting to catch up with the others, who were already outside the ship.

40

WIND WHIPPED THROUGH THE TREES, RUSTLING THE SPRUCES. SOME OF them groaned in protest. It was cold. So cold. Biting right through the sturdy fabric of Anna's blue riding shirt. Her pants were thicker, and her boots could handle the rocky dirt and spruce needles, but she could not stop the shivers.

And her hair was everywhere. She quickly dug a leather thong out of her pants pocket and tied back her blonde locks, hoping Oolaut would wait for her.

Oolaut! After so many delays, finally she would see him home. They all would.

Anna was so excited she could feel a flush actually reach her neck.

The coconut and sour smell coming off of Oolaut was stronger here. Intensely so. Stronger even than the dirt and spruce scents of the groves, or the rain-threatening smell of the harsh wind.

With her hair tied back, she could see now in the dim twilight of the Barrier.

And *what* she could see.

A field of Oolauts. A throng, a scant two hundred meters away. Hundreds of Oolauts. Thousands maybe. Not greenish like his coloring, but blue-white or gray-white, and thinner. But just as smooth. And all had the dark yellow eyes, matching the Barrier that grew just past the...

The Pillar.

Two kilometers of yellow-green rock, twisting in a gentle spiral. Smooth. Smoother than any natural rock Anna had seen anywhere on Luna. Anna's breath held in wonder. Never had she seen such a thing. Never had she been allowed to come see it, nor had any of her brothers or her sister. Father had insisted that they should not travel anywhere near it.

If not for the throng of waiting Oolauts, Anna might have stood there staring for some time.

Oolaut started forward, Dola by his side. Anna extended her strides to catch up. Edmund and Captain Barshai followed a step behind her, and Carl and Captain North seemed to linger to the rear.

A yellow-green light limned Oolaut as they walked, and flared just to the edge of blue. Some of the nearest of the throng responded in kind, though different colors. Varieties of blue or yellow or red.

Oolaut moved faster. Poor thing. Must have been excited to get home. She hurried to keep pace.

"Don't," said Dola. "Something's wrong."

"Nonsense," she said. "They're just eager to see their friend. Or maybe their relative. I'm sure he's got—"

"No. That's communication for them, and it's something I can't follow. And Oolaut knows it, but he's not translating."

"So he's pressured for time," said Captain Barshai. "Dola's right. We should hang back."

An airship flew in. Small and practical, like a thick purple tube with red fins. It landed near the throng.

"No," said Captain Barshai, and he began hustling toward the purple ship.

Anna kept pace, and she could hear North and Edmund laboring behind her.

Carl passed them all. Great long strides and fists an odd shape. As though he held something in each hand. Something she couldn't see.

Anna ran faster. Oolaut loped along beside her, and Dola kept pace with him. Captain Barshai's longer legs took him past Anna too.

The damnable unfairness of height.

"Slow, Anna," said Dola. "Oolaut asks you to slow down."

That was so unexpected that Anna slowed to a walk, her breaths heavy. And what stress had not accomplished, running did — Anna was sweating, shivering harder in the cold, unforgiving wind.

Edmund slowed too, panting for breath and shirt drenched with sweat as he ambled beside her. But Captain North ran past them, cutlass already in hand.

"No," said Anna, imploring Dola and hoping Oolaut would understand. "No. If they fight, we all lose."

Dola cocked his head at an adorable angle, apparently listening.

"Don't worry," said Edmund, catching his breath quickly enough, but shivering harder than she was. "I'm sure Mr. Jones will... Or Captain Barshai wi—"

Edmund shook his head. "I'm ready to run again if you are."

Anna nodded, but Dola said, "No!"

Anna looked down and Oolaut stepped close. Close enough to touch. Anna extended a hand and ran her fingers down what she thought of as Oolaut's neck. Smooth as petting a snake, just enough texture to excite her skin.

Oolaut glowed red, and the red glow swept over Anna, warming her.

She stopped shivering.

"Whoa," said Edmund.

"Oolaut thanks you," said Dola, "for all you have done and for all you have tried to do. And Oolaut extends this thanks to all involved. And, for now, he says goodbye."

Oolaut's body collapsed into a pile of rocks.

"No!" cried Anna, dropping to her knees, her hands frantically trying to reassemble Oolaut's body. But those rocks were nothing but chunks of Failed Site now, smoothed as though polished, and vaguely cylindrical or curved.

"He can't be..." said Edmund.

"He's not," said Dola. "Or rather, *it* is not. I'm still not sure if the concept of gender even applies."

"But," said Anna, looking into the cerulean eyes of the huge, translucent gray cat. Her tears held back, but only just. "But this was his body."

"No. This was a ... temporary form, necessary when he got stranded at the Failed Site. His own body is here, waiting for him."

From the corner of her eye, she could see the others arguing with what she presumed to be Professor Funkuro and Jakes. North still had his cutlass out, but no one else had drawn weapons as far as she could tell.

But another airship was ... no. Not just an airship. That was Father's shuttle, from the *Kiev*. She'd know that red, oblong shape anywhere, even without the Lukyanov crest.

Anna was about to say something, but before she could she noticed something else.

All the other Oolauts were gone. Vanished as though they'd never been there at all.

41

EDIK WATCHED THE RED, OBLONG SHAPE APPROACH FROM OVER THE trees and wondered, *Did Ivan Tsarevich ever have to face anything as bad as academics and wannabe noblemen?*

Even Baba Yaga herself would be a welcome sight compared to this lot.

He was standing here in the shadow of the Pillar, which filled the air with that hideous sour rum and coconut smell he would spend the next three weeks cleaning out of his clothes, on rocky dirt that was *just* slippery enough to be a real problem if it came to swordplay.

And North, of course, was more than eager to see it come to swordplay. He already had his cutlass in hand, gesturing with it like some shadow play extra. How the man had lived this long without anyone killing him was honestly beyond Edik.

If they ever managed to resolve this mess, Edik was more than tempted to leave North out here and make him walk all the way back to the Failed Site and his excuse for a ship.

Jones had something deadly concealed in his clenched fists. Edik was certain of it. But Jones' stance was as sure and confident as his voice as he assured the academics for the third time that no, they were not going to be leaving with a specimen, no matter how many there might be here at the crater's edge.

The academics. North's idea originally, but it was Edik's own damn fault for listening to him. Taking the idea in. For believing this would help against the Lukyanovs instead of inviting in the Romanovs.

As though anything could be done on this stinking excuse for a planetary body without saying "mother may I?" to one or more of the anointed few.

The academics. Professor Funkuro would have been a tall woman, if she stood straight. She had skin dark as Jones', and a shaven head polished until it gleamed. She wore a man's cut of lavender suit over a thick body.

Jakes, next to her, did not look like a Jakes. In Edik's mind, a Jakes should have been a skinny punk of a white kid, maybe with a stained tee shirt hanging over dungarees. But this Jakes had some variety of Middle-Eastern ancestry, from the skin tone and wooly brown hair and beard, and he wore a gray suit that went well with Funkuro's lavender.

"This is not a debate," said Funkuro, her Congolese accent sounding as though all her words came from the roof of her mouth, and oddly musical. "You have no authority here. A duelist and two pilots. *I* have the backing of the university, and have been guaranteed research funding from the Romanovs themselves."

"We're the ones that called you, you damned fool!" Spittle was flying again. North was on the edge of his control. "We have some say."

Jakes raised his finger, mouth open to make a point, but Funkuro silenced him with a gesture.

"No," she corrected. "You get credit for the discovery. Don't worry, we'll see that all your names get mentioned in the research papers."

"As footnotes," said Jakes, just too loud to be a mumble. Just loud enough for them all to hear, even—

"I'll carve you into a footnote!"

Funkuro pulled an amethyst pendant, on a gold chain, out of her neckline and held it up.

"Calm your man," she said in a firm voice, "or I'll calm *everyone*."

Edik glanced at Jones. Gone distant again in the eyes. God, he couldn't be thinking about killing these people could he? After his railing against murder?

Edik stepped between North and Jakes, and shoved North back with one hand.

Wait, that worked?

Edik almost stutter-stepped and lost what he was going to say. North was shorter by a good piece, but much bigger especially through the torso. Edik had some muscle too him, but he could never have just *shoved* North back...

...unless North let him.

For the first time in his life, Edik could have kissed Roger North.

"I don't care!" yelled North. "I'll gut him and mount him like a masthead. I'll—"

"You'll calm down or I'll dump your sorry ass out here." Edik made it a growl. He could only hope it was a convincing growl.

North let out a roar, but turned and stomped away.

Away around their ship.

Edik exaggerated his shrug, pulling the eyes of Funkuro and Jakes both back to him.

"He's a simple creature, really. He needs a firm hand, is all."

"The rock creature?" said Jakes.

"North," said Edik, then chuckled. Jones joined the chuckle, his arms more relaxed, but his distant eyes made the sound creepy.

But Funkuro lowered her pendant. And Edik let his eyes relax and his mind slide along thaumaturgic lines as he kept talking, looking for any other magical tricks they might be carrying.

"Here's the thing we don't think you're getting," said Edik, noting that her pendant held some version of the enchantments used on Pacifiers, which would suck all the aggression out of an opponent, "This isn't some rock creature and it isn't some kind of pet. We didn't name it Oolaut. It named *itself* Oolaut. And—"

"And any spirit one of us calls into a circle will tell us a name too," said Funkuro. "Doesn't make it on par with human life."

"But nobody called it. And it doesn't act like an elemental." Something on an anklet too. Same with Jakes, also an anklet. Department policy? "And you need—"

"You've grown attached," said Fukuro. "We see it all the time. But other spirits aren't like familiars—"

"Incoming," said Jones, voice as flat as his aspect. He was looking up at the incoming airship which, as Edik expected, bore the proud crest of the Lukyanov family.

"Who else did you call?" said Jakes, outraged. "We have a right to—"

"We told you Anna Lukyanova is with us," said Jones. "Perhaps she realized you would run to the Romanovs and called for reinforcements."

"*No!*" screamed Anna Lukyanova. She was on her knees, her hands in a crumbled ... pile ... of stone.

Oh no.

"They're all gone," said Jones. "All of them."

"What?" said Funkuro, but Edik had already turned. Already seen what Carl had seen.

Nothing but a wide, empty expanse of stone between where they stood and the Pillar. Every one of Oolaut's people. Vanished.

Funkuro whipped her head around.

"Where's North?" Not seeing him, she focused on Edik. "What did you do, Barshai? I'll—"

"You'll stop making threats," said Jones, and Edik thought it was Jones' tone more than his words that startled Funkuro back a step. "We did not do this."

"Then where's North?" said Jakes, though without any fire behind his words and his eyes wary on Jones.

"I don't know." Edik shrugged. "He might have warned them off. Couldn't blame him if he did, what with you wanting a *specimen* and all."

"Why did you call us then?" said Funkuro.

"So where is this great find?" boomed the voice of Alexei Lukyanov. He strode toward Edik and the others with his son beside him, and a dozen men armed with Pacifiers in his wake.

A dozen. Plus a fucking *Magister*.

Yes, Edik decided, he definitely would have preferred Baba Yaga.

42

No, thought Anna, this had gone far enough.

Dola had said that the pile of rock behind her was nothing to Oolaut. A temporary shell. He — and Anna was sure Oolaut was a "he" no matter what Dola said about gender — was home and safe with his people now. Back in his own body.

Magicians were supposed to be able to do that, weren't they? Travel without their bodies and return to them? Was that the same thing that Oolaut had done?

But none of those questions mattered.

Father was here.

Already she could see him exiting that shuttle, shaped like one of his cigars, only done in red. Dimi was with him, but so were a good dozen of the house guards, armed with Pacifiers that everyone could see, and hidden knives that no one could see.

The only people who had ever seen a Lukyanov guard draw his knife were either family or dead. Perhaps both. Anna would not have put that past Father at this point.

Not with him showing up ready to fight over something when he had no real idea of what he was dealing with.

Only another chance at glory. Only another chance to impede a dream of Anna's.

No. It would not come to that.

Anna marched across the rocky landscape over dirt that thinned steadily. Her boots seemed to clack louder and louder with every step. Oolaut's little gift of heat already fading under the assault of the steady winds. Anna could taste the rain they carried, but that taste was spoiled by the coconut and sour something smell.

Anna had thought the smell came from Oolaut. But apparently, if it had, it was only that Oolaut was missing the smells of home, because this whole place reeked of it.

Nerves fluttered in her stomach, but she kept her posture erect and her jaw high. If Father wished to oppose her, he would not find an obedient daughter but a woman to reckon with.

Dola was already gone, zipped past her and straight to Captain Barshai, no doubt telling him of what had occurred here. Edmund followed, a step behind her...

...and to the right.

No. That wasn't right either.

"Keep up, Edmund," she said, voice crisp. "If you intend to ask me to dinner when all this is over, and I suggest you do, you need to walk beside me like an equal, not behind me like a servant."

Edmund didn't say anything.

But he did step up to walk beside her. That brought a different flutter into Anna's stomach — a decidedly more pleasant one — but she had no time for that either.

Already Father had gathered his men. They marched toward Captain Barshai and Carl — and presumably Professor Funkuro and ... whatever title Jakes held. Father had that smile that said he was about to take charge.

Captain Barshai had one hand on the hilt of his saber. Carl had no apparent ready weapon, but looked ready to fight. Captain North...

Where was Captain North?

Anna accelerated her pace in the only acceptable fashion. She lengthened her stride. Mother would have hated to see her keep such a pace. Too masculine, she would have called the stride, and explained again the way a proper woman should walk.

Mother had never learned that there were times when a woman needed to walk like a man. Natalia Romanova had learned that lesson. And so had Anna.

"Father," she called, her voice ringing out over the wind, "two visits in one night. I feel as though I never left home."

"If you've truly left home, you will have to reimburse me for my airship."

Still smiling, but he stopped walking now. Everyone turned to look at her.

"Of course, Father," she said matching his smile, "did you think I frittered away my allowance all these years?"

Still that smile, but she could see that crinkle around his eyes. He was wondering, how much had she managed to save? How had she accomplished this with no one noticing?

Did this mean she was truly leaving?

"A matter for another time," he said with a wave of the hand. "*For when we are among family,*" he added in Russian. Then, in English, he said, "For we have gathered too many strangers to bore them with talk of finance and blood."

Twenty more meters and Anna would be there with them. She just had to hold their attention—

"Mr. Lukyanov," said Professor Funkuro, giving him the slight bow that many offered a head of a great family, "If you're hear about the find, I'm afraid I have priority."

"Pah," Father said, waving her words aside with one hand. "I know who you are, Funkuro. You are Natalia Romanova's lapdog. But your graduate student assistant, that's another matter."

Jakes took a big step away from Professor Funkuro as her eyes widened.

"Oh, yes," said Father, "and I'm sure you'll find that all records of any contact you have had about a certain find have been erased. Haven't they, Jakes?"

Jakes tilted his head and exaggerated a shrug.

"Why you sniveling little…" started Professor Funkuro, but Anna cut her off. She couldn't afford so much distraction.

"Why do we need the academics at all, Father? We are here. Natalia Romanova is not. Let us keep this in the family."

Captain Barshai held a suspicious cast to his face. Perhaps wondering how much of what she said was bluff and how much sincere.

The man had clearly never dealt with a great family before, not about anything serious.

Carl only watched Father and Dimi. No doubt ready to kill. Anna couldn't let it come to that.

"I see," said Father. He looked her up and down, reassessing her. Taking her more seriously? She could only hope. "And just what exactly is it that we wish to keep in the family, that must be discussed around strangers at all?"

"Why a new form of sentient, sapient life, of course," said a woman's voice.

A woman's voice Anna knew all too well.

Natalia Romanova stepped out from around the side of the academics' purple airship. She must have flown in with the Professor and Jakes. She wore a black cat suit with a hood up but not covering her face. In her hand she held a saber. At the end of the saber's point walked Captain North, his hands raised and his cutlass nowhere to be seen. He bled from a cut on his sword hand, and Anna noticed a trace of blood on the tip of "Aunt Natya's" saber.

Natalia Romanova raised one foot — the cat suit was thick around her feet and ankles like a pair of boots — and kicked Captain North stumbling forward. She thrust her sword, steel still naked, through a loop in the cat suit's belt.

"Now," she said, hands on her hips, "let us revisit the topic of claims and priority."

43

"LET'S NOT," SAID CARL. SO FAR, KEEPING THE DANGER-LOOK IN HIS EYE and stance had kept everyone else talking like civilized people. But the presence of Natalia Romanova changed everything.

With more than one faction of wannabe nobles involved, there could be no civilized discussion. They were all selfish and power-driven, just about the least civilized behavior Carl could imagine. So far Anna had seemed different, but she certainly knew the steps of the dance, even if she appeared to be sick of the tune.

"I've got bad news for the both of you," said Carl, looking back and forth from Lukyanov to Romanova, but keeping Lukyanov's son in view the whole time. "Neither of your houses gets to be the one to bring this news to Luna. It's already done. I've accomplished it. Check your feeds in the morning and watch the truth unfold."

"You're bluffing," said Romanova.

"You didn't forge any other links," said Lukyanov, confidently. "We had you on our scanners the entire time. We were watching."

Carl clucked his tongue and shook his head slowly, while the north wind blew stronger and colder. The bite of it excited his skin, made his nerves even more eager for action, and the first drop of rain hit his cheek. But he held still.

"Lukyanov, you disappoint me. You pretended you knew all about me, but obviously you know nothing about my past."

"I know all about your time as a spy and an assassin," he said, and Romanova nodded simply, as though it were the most obvious thing in the world.

"And do you know how people in my line of work report in while in the field? It's not as though we can go around forging links."

"I've … heard a rumor," said Dimitri Lukyanov. "Nothing official, of course, but that kind of spellwork can't be developed without word getting around, especially when it's used in an official—"

"Just tell us," said Lukyanov.

Carl raised his eyebrows at Dimitri.

"It's a variation of a memory circle. Personal to cast, difficult to maintain for long, and one reason that certain classes of spy have to be magicians." Dimitri frowned. "I'm not sure how an Initiate like you could handle the magic, but—"

"What he's trying to say," said Carl, "is that a memory circle is something a magician can use to send thoughts to another location where they're stored for him. In my line of work, I've had to use a variation for brief, one-way messages to a pre-set receiving circle where *someone else* collects the memory, if you will."

"You mustered out sixteen months ago," said Romanova, "in Tokyo. You cannot expect us to believe that the Terran Military has absorbed the cost of not only maintaining your receiving circle, but also having someone monitoring it and ready to respond *just in case* you sent another message."

"Of course not," said Carl with a small smile. "However, if you know that much about me, you know I have friends in Kennedy. And I don't mean friends the way you 'great families' mean friends. I mean guys who owe me their lives."

Carl nodded while that sank in. Neither tried to contradict him. Barshai had a small smile on his face. Must have had the same kind of friends.

"And recently," Carl continued, "I had cause to take a job for a member of a great family."

He was talking about Anna, of course, but he let his eyes suggest he might have been talking about Romanova, to give them both pause.

"And I knew that here on Luna, that meant I was going to be exposing myself to a depth of risk and politics that rivaled anything I'd ever done back in the service. So I contacted one of these friends — and I won't tell you which one — and arranged for just such a message delivery system. Just in case anything bad happened and I wanted a record. Especially on a day when I haven't had a chance to make a more conventional kind of contact since before noon."

"And you expect us," said Lukyanov, "to believe you had time to send such a detailed message?"

"Ask your boy there."

Carl's adrenaline was pumping now. His body more than ready for the fight he wasn't sure he wanted. The cold wind seemed to egg him on, holding back the rain to a few, tiny drops so far.

"Sending to a memory circle isn't difficult," said Dmitri, "but it requires concentration. Focus. Most magicians can only do it during meditation."

Edmund gasped, and Anna's mouth tightened into a line as though to bite down on a censuring remark.

But Carl had no interest in silencing Edmund. Instead he smiled.

"Something you wish to say, Edmund?"

"Well," said Edmund, his eyes jumping back and forth among everyone assembled, "Carl spent most of the flight from the Failed Site deep in meditation. Right up until that" — Edmund's eyes flicked to Barshai and back to Dmitri — "rough landing."

"It's true," said Anna, addressing her brother, who nodded.

"She's telling the truth," said Dmitri to his father. "And that would have been more than enough time. Even for an Initiate."

Carl said nothing. Just held that confident smile and hoped his bluff had worked. Oh, he did have friends in Luna who would hold such a circle for him, but the truth was he hadn't thought he'd need it.

"All right," said Romanova with a slight bow. "Let us suppose, for the sake of argument, that you have just such an arrangement and that you have already sent all your little information." She raised an eyebrow in purer condescension than Carl had ever seen before, even from Terran senators. "Between us, Alexei and I control at least two-thirds of the media outlets—"

"Including Emperor's New Clothes?"

"Ha!" said Barshai.

Emperor's New Clothes was based out of King, devoted to the idea of the truly free press. They had strict rules about the advertising they accepted, the donations, and the investments, a complex web intended to prevent anyone from gaining power over them.

They didn't have the greatest following on Luna — they couldn't compete with the sheer financial power of the outlets run by the great families — but every off-Luna outlet considered them the purest source of Lunar news. Earth, Mars — and presumably Venus — might take news from any Lunar source, but they'd give the most credence to reports from Emperor's New Clothes.

"Well played," said Romanova, with a nod. "And to which off-world corporation will this release be delivered?"

"The Terran navy," said Carl, but he'd hesitated just a moment too long. He could see it in Romanova's eyes.

She laughed, a complex sound that managed both humor and enough dismissal to make Carl's hands ache to throw the tiny blades each concealed. Barshai must have felt the same way because his sword hand twitched toward his hilt. North ground his teeth and reached for a cutlass that wasn't there.

Lukyanov's laugh followed a moment behind, a sound of contempt.

"Oh, you almost had me convinced," said Romanova. "You lie very well for a blunt instrument. But the Terran navy?" She laughed again. "Transterran Properties would have been a much better answer. Or 4M, of course."

"Speaking of 4M, do you know when Mancuso is next coming to Luna?" Lukyanov asked Romanova. "I was on Mars the last time he was here."

"Not for some time, I think. He's gone to Venus to open the new market."

"What are you doing here, Natya? Jakes should have..." Lukyanov closed his eyes and sighed. "When did you get to him?"

"A month after you did. I had to give you time to develop confidence in him."

Carl cleared his throat, drawing their eyes back to him. His only chance was to push the bluff harder.

"The choice might not have been one you agree with, the Terran navy will get word through the right channels at Earth, and you can't think they won't want to get involved."

Romanova blinked at Carl, then her eyes widened in understanding.

The laugh that followed was all humor.

"Oh, you innocent fool," she said. "Anna, I would have expected a wiser choice from you for a lover. This man believes this is about, what, credit? Academic research?"

Realization spread over Anna's face. "No," she breathed, and Carl was only just able to see her lips form the word he could not hear.

"They're gone," said Barshai. "All of them. Look around. Even the one we found earlier crumbled to base rock. It must have been a fluke phenomenon. Temporary."

"No," said Professor Funkuro. "We've been expecting to find something like this for some time now. Ever since the discovery of lacunas, elementals related to space and apparently unrelated to our traditional concept of elements—"

"Though they may related to the spirit element," said Dmitri Lukyanov.

"—pure theory and a moot point," she continued. "We had no idea that anything like lacunas were out there, but they are. And that meant that other planetary bodies were likely to have still other kinds of spirits we'd never encountered before. Spirits that might play by slightly different rules, such as the ability to form temporary bodies—"

"I get it," said Carl, while Edik said something to Dola and the gray cat familiar vanished into the ground. "Mars has carterite, the native metal that revolutionized space travel, but what does Luna have? What natural resource do you have here that no one else has?"

"Exactly," said Natalia Romanova. "These Oolauts of yours may be just the natural resource we've all been looking for. And the Romanov family stakes its claim."

44

EDIK LAUGHED. HE STOOD IN THE EXCUSE FOR A SPRINKLE THE CLOUDS had conjured up to add spice to their cold wind and laughed, head back and one hand on his stomach.

They all looked at him. Edmund's eyebrows threatened to fly right off his scalp and fly away in the wind. Anna Lukyanova's were furrowed in confusion. Funkuro looked irritated, like someone had interrupted her deep theoretical discussion with sports scores. Jakes was stepping backward, trying to disappear, perhaps.

Romanova looked as though someone had given her day-old caviar.

Lukyanov jutted his chin out, probably ready to shut Edik up. His son only raised an eyebrow, perhaps curious about where Edik was taking this.

Jones' stance didn't shift, and his eyes kept moving among Romanova, Lukyanov, and Lukyanov's son.

North joined in the laugh, even though he probably didn't know what Edik was laughing at.

"Unbelievable. If I'd known you two were going to be this easy, I'd've gone to you in the first place and started a bidding war."

In a disturbing sort of synchronicity, both Romanova and

Lukyanov shifted positions at the same time, moving their sword hands in easy reach of their weapons.

"Easy now," said Edik. "I'm just saying, if you two are ready to start some kind of house war for control of the rights to a creature neither of you has seen and no one can prove exists, I could probably have just auctioned Oolaut's remains to the highest bidder hours ago and split the proceeds among the five of us."

"The proof is going to be released by Emperor's New Clothes in the morning," said Dmitri Lukyanov. "I have no doubt that his transmission—"

"There was no transmission," said Romanova. "He was lying to us."

"Exactly!" Edik wondered if Nixia could help him steer this conversation as well as she could help him steer his ship. "And yet you two esteemed citizens of Luna have flown out here to the Pillar, perhaps the smelliest place on Luna, ready to come to blows. You even brought academics to study" — his final words came out with a laugh — "*whatever* you thought you might find."

"That will be all," said Romanova. "I've had enough of your childish games. Anka, take your attack dog and your pilots and" — she raised an eyebrow at Edmund — "whatever he is, and run along. This is a matter for adults."

"Perhaps the passage of time has not diminished your beauty, Aunt Natya, but it has succeeded in transforming me into an adult, with all accordant rights and privileges. And I have a claim of my own in this."

"Her claim," said Lukyanov stepping forward, "is the claim of my house. Whether she lives under my roof or extends the reach of my family elsewhere, she is still a Lukyanova."

"Not in this matter, Father," said Anna Lukyanova, arms folded over her stomach against a shiver that made Edik consider offering her his jacket. "In this matter I stand on my own. I will not allow you to exploit these people any more than I will allow Aunt Natya."

"The years may have initiated you into the full rights of your citizenship," said Romanova, "but they have yet to give you wisdom, Anka. You should have stood with your father in this matter. You would need his support." Her eyes flicked upwards into the wind and back, scant drops here and there on her face. "Not that his support would help you here."

"No?" said Lukyanov. "I have a dozen guards with me, Natya. What do you have?"

Romanova looked up into the wind again and smiled.

"I have *them*." She pointed.

Edik looked up. Two ships were incoming. One a huge red flying carpet with gold fringe, bearing the Romanov crest and thick enough for passengers and cargo on the inside. The other a troop transport, large and boxy and carrying the yellow crescent moon symbol of Luna.

But Luna had no military of its own. Not even a militia. Earth would never allow...

But there it was.

He hoped Dola could pull off his mission.

The purple airship with red fins, flown in by the academics, lifted off.

"Hey!" yelled Funkuro. But the ship didn't hesitate. It winged back toward Kennedy, no doubt with Jakes flying.

The flying carpet airship and the troop transport set down in the area that only recently had been full of some wondrous new form of life. Something that none of them had seen before. Not Edik or North, for all their years of flying. Not even Jones, who had been to every land and settlement humanity had managed.

All that empty space, from the promise of wonder to the promise of violence.

"You were saying something about your guards, Lyosha?" said Romanova to Lukyanov. "Or did you wish to retract your implied threat?"

"Threats and guards," said Anna Lukyanova, and her anger must have warmed her because she stood straighter now, arms down at her sides and chin raised, though the rain was beginning to sprinkle properly. "Is this what the great families are reduced to? Have you so little—"

"This is the future, Anka," said Romanova. "And the future is ever born in blood. Try to remember that."

Looking at Romanova, Edik realized he had been wrong earlier when he thought he would rather see Baba Yaga herself arrive.

She was here.

45

CARL WAS RUNNING PROBABILITIES IN HIS HEAD, AND HE DIDN'T LIKE THE answers he was getting. Twelve guards and a Magister for Lukyanov. That wasn't good, but if he could take down the Magister quickly it was possible.

But those incoming ships. Dozens of Romanov guards coming out of that ridiculous flying carpet, all with sabers and Pacifiers, and from the look of things, at least three magicians. Then there was the troop transport. No one coming out of that yet, but there would be.

If Luna was forming its own military, this was news. Maybe bigger news than Oolaut's people, at least in certain circles.

Wait. The Romanov guards had slingers too. Shaped like the pistols that no longer worked, they could "sling" tiny balls that carried spells or alchemical loads. Bad news. Worse news if they were practiced shots and carrying the *right kind* of loads. Slingers were notoriously tricky, though...

The Magister could probably counter Romanov's magicians. Might be able to take out the slingers too, if he had studied their magic at all. Lukyanov's dozen guards would be outmatched on a flat, dry surface, but this wasn't a flat, dry surface.

Here at the edge of the crater, even away from the real incline the ground sloped. The rocks were rough, with little more than a dusting of dirt, but the rain would make everything slick soon enough, turning the little dirt there was into slicks of mud.

Carl had fought in worse. But how many of these others had?

Unknown.

Plus the new arrivals would be overwhelmed for some time by the coconut and sour rum smell of the Pillar. Like fighting with a loud, constant noise in the background — not debilitating, but one more distraction coming in with every breath.

Reputation said Lukyanov could handle his sword. Odds were Romanova could as well. Plus, she was wearing a safety skinsuit, designed to reflect kinetic energy. Effective against blunt damage, certainly, and said to be good against edged weapons as well. But the thrust of a rapier? Perhaps not. Though she no doubt had the finest quality available.

Better to assume even his rapier could not pierce it.

Coming out of a skirmish alive meant supporting Lukyanov against Romanova, then opposing Lukyanov afterward.

Would the others go for it? It was certainly no guarantee of survival, much less victory.

And when to raise the question? Right now, Anna was pontificating again. Trying to get Romanova and her father to see things her way. Romanova had an indulgent smile, but she could afford it. Every second's delay bought her people more time to get into position. To acclimate to the environment.

Troops coming out of the transport now. Gray and white khaki fatigues, with just enough bluish hints to work in places as camouflage. They had swords and crossbows. No messing about with slingers. Smart. Deadly too.

Definitely not good.

This fight was a loser. But Oolaut was counting on them.

Probably, anyway. Carl wasn't sure what kind of emotions Oolaut had, or what the capabilities of its people were. But Carl wasn't ready to assume they could hide from or withstand human magic.

"Right," he said, stepping forward. He'd just cut off Anna mid-sentence, to her obvious annoyance, but logic was not going to win the day here. Not with Romanova talking about futures born in blood. That was something conquerors said, not diplomats.

"Words don't seem to have much impact on you people."

"And I imagine," said Romanova, "that you think that actions will? What actions would you take, duelist? Murder me and you won't survive the trip back to your ship. And you would accomplish nothing, because my son would take over."

"Well then—"

"Besides," she continued, louder, "if you are so keen to seek violence, perhaps there is a more *appropriate* target for you?" Romanova raised her eyebrows. "A target who has wronged you, personally, only today?"

She could not have been clearer if she had said, "Remember my offer? Kill Lukyanov. Now."

"I can think of no more appropriate choice than yourself, Natalia Romanova, and I challenge you to a—"

"Save your breath," she said. "I have no cause to duel you. You have no cause to duel me that I will recognize, and you do not have the standing to force me to accept your duel anyway." She fluttered her eyelashes. "Or did you forget that social standing in these matters makes a difference here on Luna?"

Carl's hand moved away from his sword and he hissed out a breath.

Romanova smiled.

"I have the standing," said Anna, her voice almost as cold and cutting as the wind. "And I have the cause. I was there when Oolaut was discovered. It was my action that brought him to human awareness. By law if anyone has the right to exploit this potential resource, it is I who have that right."

"A right you abrogate," said Romanova with a wave of her hand. "You have not the personal resources nor the strength of character to—"

"*I was not finished.*" Anna waited until she had Romanova's amused attention again. "The rightful claim here is mine and by social standing, mine alone. And yet you bring force of arms in an attempt to steal what is mine."

Anna stepped right up to Romanova. "I challenge you to a duel. Win and you win my claim. Lose and you and yours must withdraw."

Natalia smiled. "Very well, Anka. You wish me to pay for my supper, then so I shall. I could demand that we wait for Vladislav to fly out from my estate, but I would rather duel you myself anyway. Let us see what you have learned, little one."

"Since more than honor is at stake," said Carl, "Anna is entitled to a champion if she wishes one."

"I do." Was that relief Carl heard in her voice? "If you would be so kind, Carl. I will, of course, pay your fee."

"I will pay that fee," said Lukyanov. "You are my daughter and an insult to you is an insult to me."

"You argue over nothing," Romanova said. "Carl Jones is ineligible to stand champion."

Carl was about to deliver a sarcastic rejoinder, but then his eyes widened in realization.

"That's right," said Romanova. "Your eligibility is questionable on three counts. First, because I attempted to hire you earlier today. Second because you killed the Lukyanov champion, and Anka is a Lukyanova. But most of all—"

"I cannot, by Lunar law, fight two duels in one day." Carl kicked a loose rock into the drizzle. "Sorry, Anna, I must refuse."

"Well," said Barshai with a sigh, "I guess it better be me then."

"We—" started North, but cut himself off sharply.

"You quarreled," said Carl, "but fought no duel to completion."

"No." North shook his head, saying goodbye to his final hope of claiming that scratch on Barshai's wrist meant victory for him. "No, we were interrupted by that crash."

Only training kept the shock off Carl's face. He'd expected an argument before North would agree.

"And if the duel isn't finished," said Carl, "then it doesn't count."

He turned to Anna. "Will you accept Captain Edik Barshai as your champion?"

"I would be proud to," she said.

But Carl could see the fear hiding in her eyes.

46

"LET'S DO THIS OVER THERE," SAID EDIK, POINTING TO THE SPACE between the flying carpet Romanov airship and what seemed to be a Lunar military transport. "Maybe we can get a break from the rain."

The rain had picked up now, and with the cold wind supporting it Edik might have frozen without his nice black jacket. Anna Lukyanova was shivering nonstop now, as was Edmund. Jones looked unaffected by the weather, as though he were a golem in a purple work shirt and black slacks, not a human being at all.

Romanova's hair was plastered down by the rain, but she showed no other signs of discomfort. Edik didn't have to look to see the magic of her outfit helped her there.

Lukyanov had a coat but Edik noticed that he didn't offer that coat to his own daughter. Some father.

The rain did not touch Dmitri Lukyanov, and the moment Romanova accepted the change of location and the group turned to begin walking, Dmitri cast a spell that shielded his sister from the rain. And perhaps the cold.

It seemed that Edmund was on his own. Probably had a cold already, the way he sniffled.

Professor Funkuro must have known the same spell, because the rain didn't touch her either.

That had to be handy. Perhaps when Edik retired he'd see about furthering his thaumaturgic education.

The ground was slick underfoot. And in the dark yellow light of the Barrier, everything took on a sinister cast. Edik found his eyes flicking to every movement, as though there were more just past the corner of his eye than he could see.

This duel was not going to be fun.

Jones fell into step beside him, and murmured advice. "I assume you know the basics, but do you know what Romanova's wearing?"

"Cat suit. Can't say she doesn't have the body for it."

"Safety skinsuit. Know what that is?"

"Hey!" Edik called ahead. "You can't duel in a safety skinsuit."

"It's the only outfit I have here, and you can't force me to duel naked under these conditions. Anna Lukyanova knew what I was wearing when she issued the challenge."

Did she? Interesting question. Her eyes narrowed, but she said nothing to contradict. Was refusing to admit this sort of ignorance just one more foible of the great families of Luna?

"Technically she can wear that," said Jones, "unless this is a duel to the death. It's in bad taste though. Under other circumstances you might be able to delay things until she could change. But I think we're pushing our luck as it is."

"You have no idea," said Edik. How much longer was Dola going to need?

"What is the endpoint of this duel?" called Jones. "First blood, submission, or death?"

"First blood," said Anna.

"All right," said Jones, voice low. "Romanova's probably counting on the suit for perfect protection, but there are two things she might not realize. I'm going to make a big deal about one until she accepts it. The other, though, is that every safety skinsuit is weaker at the seams. Aim for joints where you can, especially under the arms."

"Hey," said Edik, raising the other objection before Jones could, just to remind the professional duelist that Edik had, in fact, been around the system a few times himself. "If this is to first blood, standard safety skinsuit rules apply. If I hit hard enough to get my sword knocked backward, it counts as a cut."

"Agreed," she said without slowing her pace. "Provided three judges agree unanimously. Jones, Lyosha, and Funkuro."

"The code says nothing about—"

"This isn't Kennedy. There's not an unbiased witness out here, and we certainly don't have anyone from the Fair Arbiter's Guild. You want the skinsuit rules, you accept this."

"Done," said Edik.

Edik delayed things as much as he could. He questioned the footing, changed the spot three times, asked about a rain shield from the Magister (who either couldn't or wouldn't provide one), demanded that they review all the ground rules twice, and made a big deal about stretching first.

But Dola wasn't back yet, and Romanova was getting impatient.

And every time she got impatient, Edik would have sworn that those — Lunar soliders? — raised their crossbows.

Finally, Edik could delay no longer, and the duel began.

Ten meters of space between the red flying carpet airship — a good four meters tall and probably twenty long — and the boxy gray troop transport. The ground was sloped and Edik had the high ground, but Romanova didn't seem concerned.

The guards and troops all formed a perimeter around the two ships, hemming Edik and Romanova into the channel between those two ships.

No leading her on a chase then. There went one of Edik's strategies.

Jones, Anna Lukyanova, North, Edmund, and Funkuro watched from atop the flying carpet. Lukyanov and his son watched from atop the troop transport.

Romanova saluted, giving Edik no choice but to respond. Her saber was a Dalca, much higher quality than Edik's, which didn't even have a maker's mark.

They stood only four strides apart. She might as well have been in stabbing distance.

Her stance was balanced and wide, her left hand hanging ignored behind her. Her wrist looked relaxed. Her face looked relaxed. Even her legs looked relaxed.

Edik was anything but relaxed. His grip was too tight on his saber. His knees jittered. His heart pounded. The rain coming down half-blinded him. His breaths were kicking snot out of his nostrils with each rapid flare.

Her first step was measured. Gauging.

Edik screamed and leaped forward, slashing back and forth with his sword and sliding on the slick rocks.

Romanova dove to the side, but her attempt at a roll turned into an awkward slip toward the troop transport.

Edik tried to stop. To come after her. But his boots couldn't find an edge to grip.

Romanova found her feet first. Coming down at him in a controlled standing skid. Almost skiing on the mud-slicked rocks. Her sword thrust forward like a prow.

Finally Edik hit something hard. The boot of a guard, trying to kick him back into the fight.

The guard slipped and fell, but Edik got to one foot and his knee.

Sword coming at his face. Edik parried hard and slipped-rolled right before her next attack cut him.

A cry. She'd cut a soldier. Sword tangled in his uniform. Romanova pulled back, tugging.

Edik tried a controlled skid at her. Sword forward.

Romanova cut free. Sword back in line in time to parry.

But Edik had momentum. Plowed into her. Skinsuit shoved him back. Two more cuts, both parried.

They faced off against each other. Two paces apart, but paces weren't easy here.

The guards eased back to give them room. Rain pounded down harder than before.

Edik slip-stepped a pace closer. When her attack came he blocked and sprang at her again, free arm low and reaching past her.

His shoulder hit her gut. The skinsuit threw him back.

Edik's hand caught Romanova behind the knee. He yanked.

Down she came, sword arm wide.

Edik landed on top of her, skinsuit throwing them both up. But his sword in position. Ready to cut that arrogant face—

"Enough," said a voice that reverberated across the whole area of the Pillar. Edik was thrown back from Romanova.

He swore and raised his sword, turning to see who had interfered. And how.

Dola stood in the center of the dueling area. Glowing that dark yellow, like the Barrier.

Like Oolaut.

All the surrounded guards fell unconscious, all at once.

Standing over them were Oolaut's people. A ring at least eight rows thick.

"I speak for the Rhian people," said Dola in that voice so unlike his own that it sent chills down Edik's spine that had nothing to do with the rain and cold. This voice was hollow, and too deep. "I speak with their voice, tell you their words."

"You mean..." started Edik, but his words died away.

Dola didn't even feel like Dola right now. He couldn't feel his connection to his own familiar, and the shock seized something inside his chest.

"You have met one of the Rhian today. Known to you as Oolaut. Some of you assisted him. For that we are grateful. However, we are no one's possessions to hoard or resources to exploit. None may duel for us and none may stand for us."

"Well," started Romanova, but Dola wasn't listening.

"We declare that we stand for ourselves and represent ourselves. Look to your army." Dola paused while Romanova and Lukyanov looked at their guards. "They live because we wish it. We have no wish to harm you. But you will leave now. And you will leave without slaves and without specimens."

"What about friends?" said Anna Lukyanova.

"Let all who would own or exploit us leave now or face our wrath."

Edik wasn't sure what their wrath entailed, but there were certainly a lot of them. And they seemed to have some facility with magic. Edik didn't know of any magician who could have disabled so many armed men and women so quickly without an obvious pulse of magic.

"This is not over," said Romanova, while her guards and soldiers groaned back to consciousness. She looked up at Anna Lukyanova. "Did you hear me..."

She went on for a moment, but Edik wasn't listening. He was over on his knees in front of Dola, who was shaking his head hard enough to ruffle all his fur.

"You in there, buddy?" said Edik.

"Yeah," said Dola, voice weak, but strong enough to send a wash of relief from Edik's rain-soaked head to his sweat-soaked socks. "But I'm going to need a week-long bath to feel clean again."

Edik dropped his saber and snatched his familiar up in his arms.

47

FATHER WAS NOT HAPPY ABOUT LEAVING, AND NEITHER WAS NATALIA Romanova. She left without another word, but Anna had seen such a dark look in the woman's eye before. Not aimed at herself, but at a slight by the Pajari family.

Not long after, the Pajari's import-export business lost a major contract. Natalia Romanova had never said a word, but the message had not been lost on the other great families — anger the Romanovs at your peril.

But to Hell with Natalia Romanova. She had to learn that there were limits, even for a great family of Luna.

Father had to learn that as well. Anna had no idea whether or not the day's events had even begun to sink in for him. She could not quite read the look in his eye when he said goodbye.

But then, just before he turned away, he smiled. Only a bare movement to his lips and a glint in those ice blue eyes of his. But it was enough. Anna knew. He might not have agreed with her decisions — especially what he may or may not have believed about her and Carl, and most of all her decision to leave home — but Father was proud of how she conducted herself here today, in the shadow of the Pillar.

After so very many years of trying, she had finally shown him something to be proud of. Some day he might even admit it.

Dimi had embraced her, and ruffled her sopping hair, and kissed her forehead before he left. And then he had done one other thing. He had waved his hands and a blast of air and heat had blown the water and cold right out of her. Then he winked and hurried after Father.

Her hair hung wild, but she stood dry and warm in the center of that downpour, Dimi's rain shield ensuring she stayed that way.

And then the other airships were away, and only she, Carl, poor sniffling Edmund, Dola, and Captains Barshai and North remained with the Oolauts.

No, with the Rhian people.

One of the Rhian stepped forward, its movements swifter and surer than Oolaut's had been in the body it pulled out of the rock of the Failed Site. It seemed entirely untroubled by the rain and mud. Its eyes, like all the Rhian eyes she'd seen so far, were the same dark yellow shade as the Barrier...

Anna turned and stared at the Pillar. Huge, twisting green and yellow rock, but smooth. Not rough like all the natural rocks seemed to be here on Luna.

The Rhian people were smooth like that too. And their eyes...

There was something there. Something on the tip of Anna's mind, if only she could put the pieces together.

"Oolaut says thank you," said Dola.

"That's" — Edmund sneezed — "Tha's Oolaut?"

"Yes," said Dola, and Oolaut moved up to Edmund and pressed that tapering nose to the center of Edmund's chest.

Carl's eyes widened. So did the eyes of both captains.

"Whoa," said Edmund. "Thanks." He still had something of a sniffle, but he'd stopped shivering. And the rain didn't seem to both him so much now.

"Oolaut says that should last an hour. More than enough time to do what needs to be done before we're all on our way."

"Just what needs to be done?" asked Captain North in a dark tone.

"With Edik's permission," said Dola, "I would like to offer Oolaut my voice for a few minutes."

Captain Barshai nodded, but his lips stretched in a frown that said he wasn't happy about this. Anna couldn't understand why that was.

"We have hidden," said Dola in the same hollow, deep voice as when he'd spoken for the Rhian earlier, "since your people came here. Even after we took bodies. You ways are strange. And you keep slaves." Oolaut looked at Captain Barshai and nodded. "Most of you, anyway. Some, it seems, have moved beyond that."

Oolaut looked back toward the direction that Father's and Natalia Romanova's ships had flown.

"But some push beyond even that. We will not have it. We will not tolerate it."

"How will you stop it?" asked Carl.

"We are not without power of our own. And this place is ours. Ever were we here, before even your kind arrived. We know the secrets of your survival, and we know how to dismantle them."

Oolaut looked up at the Barrier. The captains both uttered sounds of surprise, but Carl simply nodded, as though it made perfect sense to him.

Anna wasn't quite that confident, but she understood too. These Rhian, they had something to do with that Barrier. She could believe they could take it down.

"But we have no wish to do that. We have no wish to harm any of you. And so we seek another way. We must have a voice. We must have an emissary who would speak for us to your people. Learn our ways and help us find a path to live together."

"Me," said Anna, raising her hand. "I'll do it. I'm not a magician. I couldn't possibly try to bind your people or work any magic against you. But I have the right name and the right family to make people listen. If I tell them that I speak with your voice, they will listen to me."

"Before you can speak for us, you must learn to listen to us."

"I'll find a way. There has to be one."

"This might require a magician," said Captain Barshai, in surprisingly gentle tones, but glancing over at Carl meaningfully. "Working with spirits is part of our trade."

"No," said Oolaut. "We favor working with one who cannot bind us. Anna Lukyanova, if you will come here on your own, we will work with you until you hear us. Then your work can truly begin."

"Not a lot of money in this kind of work," said Carl.

"Money isn't everything," said Anna.

"Spoken like someone who've never been short of it," said Captain Barshai.

"The Grand Council of Luna will give me a stipend, I'm certain. And the universities will pay to have me speak to them. And I'm not without some money of my own."

"I can help you work the numbers," said Edmund. "And get some grants. I'm sure there are foundations just waiting for a chance to throw money at something like this."

"Then it's settled?" Anna asked, addressing her question somewhere between Dola and Oolaut.

"This is acceptable to the Rhian people."

"Excellent," and Anna did something that a Lukyanova should not have done in front of so many people who weren't family.

She pumped her fist in triumph.

48

EDIK LEFT NIXIA TO HANDLE THE FLYING, AND FETCHED A PLATE OF turkey and Swiss cheese sandwiches from the galley, along with a bottle of cognac. He carried it all on a ceramic platter back into the main cabin where his passengers slumped, exhausted, in their seats. Dola even stretched out, belly up and paws in the air, at the forward end of the cabin.

Entirely unfair, thought Edik, that he was the one fetching food and drinks when he — not any of them — had been the one to fight a duel in the rain and mud and slippery rocks near the Pillar.

But then, he would have been damned before he let any of them down into the private parts of the ship. The main cabin head had to suffice for them to clean themselves up after running around in that rainstorm, while Edik used his personal head for a more thorough job.

"Thank God," said Jones, talking with his mouth full of whole wheat, turkey, Swiss cheese and lettuce, tucking in like he hadn't seen a meal in days.

"You're a lifesaver," said Edmund.

Anna Lukyanova and North offered simpler, but no less sincere thanks.

Edik had to admit that his own sandwich tasted straight from heaven.

"Hell of a day," said Edik, then to Jones he said, "Think Romanova's still paying for all this flying?"

"Definitely," said Anna Lukyanova, and when they looked at her, she continued. "Normally her majordomo would probably haggle you down some, or nit-pick your expenses, just to remind you who's in charge. But she's not going to want me to get word that she shorted my friend on a bill. Not when she hears what my new title is."

Friend?

The shock must have shown on Edik's face, because she smiled.

"After what we all went through today, if we're not friends I think there's something wrong with us."

"Even me?" asked North. Which was good, because Edik would have felt petty if the question had come from him.

"Even you." She arched an eyebrow and hesitated before the next bite of her sandwich. "Provided you stop coming on to me. That's never going to happen."

North didn't say anything. He barely nodded in response, though he did nod. Suddenly he looked at Jones.

"What about you and me. We been crossed a couple times today."

"I was in the service a number of years," said Jones, and Edik tuned out of the rest. But the gist of it seemed to be that North stood tall when it mattered, and that was enough for Jones.

North didn't ask Edik, and that was probably for the best.

"Think they really could have taken down the Barrier?" said North, when devout eating caused a lull in the conversation. "Just ripped it down?"

"They were in the best possible place to do it," said Jones.

That brought the slow head turn from everyone else in the room. Even Dola.

Apparently Edik had to be the one to ask.

"Why is the Pillar the best possible place?"

"That's right," said Jones. "Technically that's probably a secret, isn't it?" He shrugged. "Well, if so no one ever told me *officially*. Still, keep this to yourselves. The Pillar is the site where the Barrier was first cast. The spells have been refined over the years, and the actual physical location where they repeat the spell and handle the alchemy is underground—"

"*That's it!*" yelled Anna Lukyanova, leaping to her feet, so excited that Edik could actually see a little color in her cheeks. "The Pillar. That's some kind of result of alchemical waste. Isn't it?"

"Something like that," said Jones. "Something to do with the early alchemical blends being off, and the way the corrections didn't quite fit together for a while—"

"That's where they came from." Anna Lukyanova smacked her palm. "That's why they have bodies. We changed the lunar surface there. Made it hospitable to the Rhian while we were making the rest of Kennedy hospitable to ourselves."

"So these things," said North, "I mean these *people* will be everywhere there's a Barrier?"

"No!" She was pacing now. "The subsequent Barriers didn't go up until the first one was perfected. And by then, you no longer had the interaction of past attempts pulling together..."

She stopped and stood straight.

"I need the formulae," she said. "If I could study the different formulae used, and the changes, and consult someone who could puzzle through the thaumaturgy involved, maybe I could figure out how they made their bodies."

"Slow down," said Jones. "This is an interesting theory, Anna, but the moment you voice it you won't be able to control access to the Rhian."

"She doesn't now," said Dola. "The Rhian control their own access. She'll just be—"

"Point is," said Jones, "you'll be dealing with competition from a thousand angles."

"He may have a point," said Edik. "The more people find out about the combination of phenomena that led to the Rhian, the more people will dig into their nature from different angles. They'll experiment. Might not end well."

"People will figure it out anyway," said North with a shrug. "Not like Jones here is the only one who knows what the Pillar is."

Anna Lukyanova dropped back down in her seat, then sat up straight again.

"Doesn't matter. Figuring this out will help. I know it will. I'll just have to go about it carefully."

"Well, at least let me put you in touch with a Journeyman who knows how to keep his mouth shut," said Jones.

"Look," said Edik, pouring out cognac into shot glasses, which were all he kept apart from normal drinking glasses. "Maybe you're right about their history. Maybe you're not. Either way, that's a problem for another day, all right? Right now let's drink a toast."

He handed out the drinks and waited until everyone held a shot glass aloft with the amber drink aloft. It was as fine a cognac as Edik could afford — which probably meant that it wasn't as good as what the Lukyanov's gave their servants — and Edik savored the rich, sweet scent.

"*Vashe zrodovye*," he said, and against all normal rules of cognac — but not all rules of toasts, especially among tour ship captains — he slammed down the delightful taste, feeling the burn the whole way down.

Jones and North both slammed theirs — and to Edik's surprise, so did Anna Lukyanova — but Edmund couldn't quite handle it. He choked and coughed a bit, and had to settle for three swallows to finish.

Anna Lukyanova poured another round, saying, "Life is very good to drink to, especially after a day like today, but if you don't mind I have another toast I'd prefer."

Everyone held their glasses aloft.

"*Za sbychu mecht!*"

They slammed their drinks once more — Edmund managed in two swallows this time — and Edik was already starting to feel a pleasant warmth spreading through him.

"What did that mean?" asked North.

"The grammar of it is terrible," Anna Lukyanova said with a

smile. If she was feeling the cognac at all, Edik couldn't tell. "But it essentially means, may all our dreams come true."

Jones looked away out a porthole. Edmund tried not to look at Anna Lukyanova. But North looked over at Edik, and then away. Guilt, no doubt. Probably finally feeling the guilt of his fare-stealing ways.

Well, let him feel his guilt, as long as he didn't lament it long and loud.

Right now, Edik felt too good to listen.

"Say, Barshai," said North.

Edik sighed and glanced at Dola, who stared back with feline mirth in his eyes. Edik didn't want to ask. He wanted to go check something on the bridge. Or hit the head. Or just drink some more cognac. Anything but ask.

"Never mind," said North, shaking his head hard enough to shake that scraggly beard. "'s nothing."

"You two still going to fight that duel in a couple of days?" said Jones.

"No!" said Edmund. "We're all friends, now. Right? Friends don't duel each other."

"Happens more often than you'd think," said Jones.

North was looking at Edik again, something clearly on his mind. Edik bit his cheek, then made himself say, "Out with it, North. What's on your mind?"

"Just thinking." North looked down. "Seeing things from your side. Might be, just might be you've got some cause to get angry. Might be, looked at from a certain angle, you could maybe see what I did as stealing your fares. Even though they ain't paid you yet."

Edik started to say something, but Jones silenced him with a gesture, his eyes intent on North, who still had more to say.

"So I was thinkin', maybe, what if you and me split those fares from this morning?"

"And the tips?" said Edik, shocking throwing the words past his lips before his mind could even think them.

North gritted his teeth but said, "All right. And the tips."

"No," said Edik, shaking his head slowly. Dola got to his feet and trotted over while Edik kept talking. "No, you keep the tips. If they liked your service, then you deserve what they gave you."

The only sound Edik could hear was Dola's proud purr. Everything else in the cabin had gone still, the others watching them.

"In fact," said North, "I was thinking. Know what makes more money than one tour ship? Two tour ships. And yours can go places mine can't. So what if we, you and me, what if we—"

"—formed a partnership?" said Edik, suspicion in his voice. "I don't know..."

"Think about it." North was gaining a little momentum now, perhaps bolstered by Edik's failure to shoot the idea out of the sky. "We could add shorter flights, and more of them, opening up a new market."

"And I could extend my tours to cover more ground. Maybe even pick up from different cities. Maybe even add travel-tour packages."

"Could be good."

Suddenly Edmund jumped to his feet. "And until you can trust each other you can trust me!"

Edik started laughing, and so did North, and everyone else followed.

"All right, you pirate," said Edik. "Let's give it a shot."

Edik and North shook hands.

SIGN UP FOR STEFON'S NEWSLETTER

Stefon loves to keep in touch with his readers, and loves to keep you reading. The best way for him to do both is for you to sign up for his newsletter.

Sign up at http://www.stefonmears.com/join

If you sign up for Stefon's newsletter, you get...

- Monthly updates about his publishing and travel schedules
- His latest news, in brief, and answers to reader questions
- A free short story for signing up
- List-only offers and occasional specials
- Plus a free short story every month!

ABOUT THE AUTHOR

Stefon Mears knows where to find the heart of Koschei the Deathless. Stefon has more than thirty books to his credit, and he never stops writing. He earned his M.F.A. in Creative Writing from N.I.L.A., and his B.A. in Religious Studies (double emphasis in Ritual and Mythology) from U.C. Berkeley. He's a lifelong gamer and fantasy fan. Stefon lives in Portland, Oregon, with his wife and three cats.

Look for Stefon online:
www.stefonmears.com
himself@stefonmears.com